SONS

'MIDNIGHT SONS and the men of Alaska started all this craziness, but the men of Promise refuse to be outdone. They're just as stubborn, just as ornery, just as proud. And just as lovable. Come to Promise—if you're like me, you'll never want to leave!'

Enjoy

Debbie Macomber

Debbie loves to hear from her readers. You can reach her at P.O. Box 1458, Port Orchard, Washington 98366 USA.

WATCH OUT FOR MORE STORIES FROM PROMISE!

Dr. Texas

Nell's Cowboy

Lone Star Baby

THE PEOPLE OF PROMISE: CAST OF CHARACTERS

Nell Bishop: thirty-something widow with a son, Jeremy, and a daughter, Emma. Her husband died in a tractor accident.

Ruth Bishop: Nell's mother-in-law. Lives with Nell and her two children.

Dovie Boyd: runs an antiques shop and has dated Sheriff Frank Hennessey for ten years.

Caroline Daniels: postmistress of Promise.

Maggie Daniels: Caroline's five-year-old daughter.

Dr. Jane Dickinson: new doctor in Promise.

Ellie Frasier: owner of Frasier's Feed Store.

Frank Hennessey: local sheriff.

Max Jordan: owner of Jordan's Towne & Country.

Wade McMillen: preacher of Promise Christian Church.

Edwina and Lily Moorhouse: sisters. Retired schoolteachers.

Cal and Glen Patterson: local ranchers. Brothers.

Phil and Mary Patterson: parents of Cal and Glen. Operate a local B&B.

Louise Powell: town gossip.

Wiley Rogers: sixty-year-old foreman at the Weston ranch.

Laredo Smith: wrangler hired by Savannah Weston.

Barbara and Melvin Weston: mother and father to Savannah, Grady and Richard. The Westons died six years ago.

Richard Weston: youngest of the Weston siblings.

Savannah Weston: Grady and Richard's sister.

Grady Weston: oldest of the Weston siblings.

DEBBIE MACOMBER

CAROLINE'S CHILD

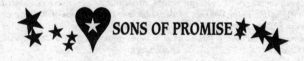 SONS OF PROMISE

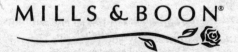

MILLS & BOON®

First published in Great Britain 1999
Harlequin Mills & Boon Limited,
Eton House, 18-24 Paradise Road, Richmond, Surrey TW9 1SR

© Debbie Macomber 1998

ISBN 0 263 81500 5

Set in Times Roman 10½ on 11½ pt.
02-9903-50014 C1

Printed and bound in Norway
by AIT Trondheim AS, Trondheim

Chapter One

Clutching the mail in one hand, Grady Weston paced the narrow corridor inside the post office. He glanced distractedly at the row of mailboxes, gathering his courage before he approached Caroline Daniels, the postmistress.

His tongue felt as if it'd wrapped itself around his front teeth, and he was beginning to doubt he'd be able to utter a single sensible word. It shouldn't be so damned difficult to let a woman know he found her attractive!

"Grady?" Caroline's voice reached out to him.

He spun around, not seeing her. Great. Not only was he dreaming about her, now he was hearing her voice.

"Open your box," she instructed.

He fumbled for the key and twisted open the small rectangular door, then peered in. Sure enough, Caroline was there. Not all of her, just her brown eyes, her pert little nose and lovely mouth.

If he'd possessed his brother's gift for flattery, Grady would have said something clever. Made some flowery remark. Unfortunately all he managed was a gruff unfriendly-sounding "Hello."

"Hi."

Caroline had beautiful eyes, dark and rich like freshly brewed coffee, which was about as poetic as Grady got. Large and limpid, they reminded him of a calf's, but he figured that might not be something a woman wanted to hear, even if *he* considered it a compliment. This was the problem, Grady decided. He didn't know how to talk to a woman. In fact, it'd been more than six years since he'd gone out on an actual date.

"Can I help you with anything?" she asked.

He wanted to invite her to lunch, and although that seemed a simple enough request, he couldn't make himself ask her. Probably because their relationship so far hadn't been too promising. Calling it a "relationship" wasn't really accurate, since they'd barely exchanged a civil word and had never so much as held hands. Mostly they snapped at each other, disagreed and argued—if they were speaking at all. True, they'd danced once; it'd been nice, but only when he could stop worrying about stepping on her toes.

Who was he kidding? Holding Caroline in his arms had been more than nice, it had been *wonderful.* In the month since, he hadn't been able to stop thinking about that one dance. Every night when he climbed into bed and closed his eyes, Caroline was there to greet him. He could still feel her softness against him, could almost smell the faint scent of her cologne. The dance had been ladies' choice, and that was enough to let him believe—hope—she might actually hold some regard for him, too. Despite their disagreements, *he'd* been the one she'd chosen to ask.

"You had lunch yet?" Grady asked, his voice brusque. He didn't mean to sound angry or unfriendly. The timbre of his voice and his abrupt way of speaking had caused him plenty of problems with Maggie, Caroline's five-year-old daughter. He'd been trying to get in the kid's good graces for months now, with only limited success. But he'd tried. He hoped Caroline and Maggie gave him credit for that.

Caroline's mouth broke into a wide grin. "Lunch? Not yet, and I'm starved."

Grady spirits lifted considerably. "Well, then, I was

thinking, seeing as I haven't eaten myself…'' The words stumbled all over themselves in his eagerness to get them out. "You want to join me?"

"Sure, but let me get this straight. Is this an invitation, as in a date?"

"No.'' His response was instinctive, given without thought. He'd been denying his feelings for her so long that his answer had come automatically. He feared, too, that she might misread his intentions. He was attracted to Caroline and he wanted to know her better, but beyond that—he wasn't sure. Hell, what he knew about love and marriage wouldn't fill a one-inch column of the *Promise Gazette*.

Some of the happiness faded from her smile. "Understood. Give me a few minutes and I'll meet you out front." She moved out of his range of vision.

Grady closed the box, but left his hand on the key. How could anyone with the skills to run a thriving cattle ranch in the Texas Hill Country be such a fool when it came to women?

He rapped on the post-office box hard enough to hurt his knuckles. "Caroline!" Then he realized he had to open the box. He did that, then stared through it and shouted for her a second time. "Caroline!"

Her face appeared, eyes snapping with impatience. "What's the rush?' she demanded. "I said it'd take me a few minutes.''

The edges of the post box cut into his forehead and chin and knocked his Stetson askew. "This *is* a date, all right?"

She stared back at him from the other side, and either she was overwhelmed by his offer to buy her lunch or surprised into speechlessness.

"All right?" he repeated. "This is a date."

She continued to look at him. "I shouldn't have asked,'' she finally said.

"I'm glad you did.'' And he was. He could think of no

better way to set things straight. He hadn't invited her to lunch because he needed someone to pass the time with; if that was what he'd wanted, he could have asked his sister, Savannah, or her husband or Cal Patterson—or any number of people. No, he'd asked Caroline because he wanted to be with *her.* For once he longed to talk to her without interference or advice from his matchmaking sister. It didn't help to have Maggie there hiding her face in her mother's lap every time he walked into the room, either. This afternoon it'd be just the two of them. Caroline and him.

Grady respectfully removed his hat when she joined him in the lobby.

"This is a pleasant surprise," Caroline said.

"I was in town, anyway." He didn't mention that he'd rearranged his entire day for this opportunity. It was hard enough admitting that to himself, let alone Caroline.

"Where would you like to eat?" he asked. The town had three good restaurants: the café in the bowling alley; the Chili Pepper, a Texas barbecue place; and a Mexican restaurant run by the Chavez family.

"How about Mexican Lindo?" Caroline suggested.

It was the one he would have chosen himself. "Great."

Since the restaurant was on Fourth Avenue, only two blocks from the post office, they walked there, chatting as they went. Or rather, Caroline chatted and he responded with grunts and murmurs.

Grady had long ago realized he lacked the ability to make small talk. Unlike his younger brother, Richard, who could charm his way into—or out of—anything. Grady tried not to feel inadequate, but he was distinctly relieved when they got to the restaurant.

In a few minutes they were seated at a table, served water and a bowl of tortilla chips along with a dish of extra-hot salsa. He reached for a chip, scooped up as much salsa as it would hold and popped it in his mouth. He ate another and then another before he noticed that Caroline hadn't touched a single chip.

He raised his eyes to hers and stopped chewing, his mouth full.

Caroline apparently read the question in his eyes. "I don't eat corn chips," she explained. "I fill up on them and then I don't have room for anything else."

He swallowed and nodded. "Oh."

A moment of silence passed, and Grady wondered if her comment was a subtle hint that she was watching her weight. From what he understood, weight was a major preoccupation with women. Maybe she was waiting for him to tell her she shouldn't worry about it; maybe he was supposed to say she looked great. She did. She was slender and well proportioned, and she wore her dark brown hair straight and loose, falling to her shoulders. In his opinion she looked about as perfect as a woman could get. Someday he'd tell her that, but not just yet. Besides, he didn't want her to think he was only interested in her body, although it intrigued him plenty. He admired a great deal about her, especially the way she was raising Maggie on her own. She understood the meaning of the words responsibility and sacrifice, just like he did.

She was staring at him as if she expected a comment, and Grady realized he needed to say something. "You could be fat and I'd still have asked you to lunch."

Her smooth brow crumpled in a puzzled frown.

"I meant that as a compliment," he sputtered, and decided then and there it was better to keep his trap shut. Thankfully the waitress came to take their order. Grady decided on chicken enchiladas; Caroline echoed his choice.

"This is really very nice," she said, and reached for the tall glass of iced tea.

"I wanted us to have some time alone," he told her.

"Any particular reason?"

Grady rested his spine against the back of his chair and boldly met her look. "I like you, Caroline." He didn't know any way to be other than direct. This had gotten him into difficulties over the years. Earlier that spring he'd taken a dislike to Laredo Smith and hadn't been shy about letting his sister and everyone else know his feelings. But he'd been wrong in his assessment of the man's character. Smith's truck had broken down and Savannah had brought him home to the ranch. Over Grady's objections she'd hired him herself, and before long they'd fallen in love. It came as a shock to watch his sane, sensible sister give her heart to a perfect stranger. Still, Grady wasn't proud of the way he'd behaved. By the time Laredo decided it'd be better for everyone concerned if he moved on, Grady had wanted him to stay. He'd gone so far as to offer the man a partnership in the ranch in an effort to change his mind. Not that it'd done any good. To Grady's eternal gratitude, Laredo had experienced a change of heart and returned a couple of months later. Love had driven him away, but it had also brought him back.

Savannah and Laredo had married in short order and were now involved in designing plans for their own home, plus raising quarter horses. Savannah, with her husband's active support, continued to grow the antique roses that were making her a name across the state.

In the weeks since becoming his brother-in-law, Laredo Smith had proved himself a damn good friend and Grady's right-hand man.

"I like you, too," Caroline said, but she lowered her gaze as she spoke, breaking eye contact. This seemed to be something of an admission for them both.

"You do?" Grady felt light-headed with joy. It was all he could do not to leap in the air and click his heels.

"We've known each other a lot of years."

"I've known you most of my life," he agreed, but as he said the words, he realized he didn't *really* know Caroline. Not the way he wanted, not the way he hoped he would one day. It wasn't just that he had no idea who'd fathered Maggie; apparently no one else in town did, either. He wondered what had attracted her to this man, why she hadn't married him. Or why he'd left her to deal with the pregnancy and birth alone. It all remained a mystery. Another thing Grady didn't understand about Caroline were the changes in her since her daughter's birth. In time Grady believed she'd trust him enough to answer his questions, and he prayed he'd say and do the right thing when she did.

Their lunches arrived and they ate, stopping to chat now and then. The conversation didn't pall, but again he had to credit Caroline with the skill to keep it going. Half an hour later, as he escorted her back to the post office, Grady was walking on air.

"I'll give you a call tomorrow," he said, watching her for some sign of encouragement. "If you want," he added, needing her reassurance.

"Sure."

Her response was neither encouraging nor discouraging.

"I'd like to talk to Maggie again, if she'll let me."

"You might try this afternoon, since she's spending the day with Savannah."

This was news to Grady, but he'd been busy that morning and had left the house early. He hadn't spoken to Savannah other than a few words over breakfast, and even if he'd known Maggie was staying with his sister, he wouldn't have had time to chat with the girl that morning.

"I'll make a point of saying hello," he said. His heart lifted when it suddenly struck him that he'd be seeing Caroline again later in the day, when she came to pick up Maggie.

They parted. Whistling, Grady sauntered across the asphalt parking lot toward his truck. He felt damn good. The afternoon had gone better than he'd hoped.

He was about to open the cab door when Max Jordan stopped him.

"Grady, have you got a moment?" The older man, owner of the local Western-wear store, quickened his pace.

"Howdy, Max." Grady grinned from ear to ear and didn't let the somber expression on Max's face get him down. "What can I do for you?"

Max shuffled his feet a couple of times, looking uncomfortable. "You know I hate to mention this a second time, but Richard still hasn't paid me for the clothes he bought three months ago."

The happy excitement Grady had experienced only moments earlier died a quick death. "It was my understanding Richard mailed you a check."

"He told me the same thing, but it's been more than two weeks now and nothing's come. I don't feel I should have to wait any longer."

"I don't think you should, either. I'll speak to him myself," Grady promised.

"I hate to drag you into this," Max muttered, and it was clear from his shaky voice how much the subject distressed him.

"Don't worry about it, Max. I understand."

The older man nodded and turned away. Grady climbed into his truck and clenched the steering wheel with both hands as the anger flooded through him. Leave it to his brother to lie and cheat and steal!

What infuriated Grady was that he had no one to blame but himself. He'd allowed Richard to continue living on the Yellow Rose. Allowed him to tarnish the family name. Allowed himself to believe, to hope, that the years away had changed his brother.

All his illusions had been shattered. They were destroyed like so much else Richard had touched. He'd done his damnedest to ruin Grady, and he'd come close. But Richard had succeeded in ruining his own life—his potential to be a different person, a worthwhile human being.

Charming and personable, a born leader, Richard could have accomplished great things. Instead, he'd used his charisma and personality to swindle others, never understanding that the person he'd cheated most had been himself.

Six years earlier Richard had forged Grady's signature and absconded with the cash their parents had left—cash that would have paid the inheritance taxes on the ranch and covered the burial expenses. Grady and Savannah had found themselves penniless following the tragedy that had claimed their parents' lives. It'd taken six long back-breaking frustration-filled years to crawl out of debt. Grady had sacrificed those years to hold on to the ranch while Richard had squandered the money. When it had run out, he'd returned home with his tail between his legs, looking for a place to stay until he received a severance check from his last job—or so he'd said.

Deep down Grady had wanted to believe in Richard. His sister had begged him to let their younger brother stay. But she didn't need to beg very hard or very long for him to relent. Unfortunately it had become apparent that a liar and a cheat didn't change overnight—or in six years. Grady's brother was the same now as the day he'd stolen from his family.

Despite the air conditioner, the heat inside the truck cab sucked away Grady's energy. It should have come as no surprise to discover that Richard had lied to him again. This time would be the last, Grady vowed.

Oh, yes, this episode was the proverbial last straw.

HIS DAYS IN PROMISE were numbered, Richard Weston thought as he sat on his bed in the bunkhouse. It wouldn't be long before Grady learned the truth. The whole uncomfortable truth. Actually he was surprised he'd managed to hold out this long; he credited that to his ability to lie effectively. But then, small-town folks were embarrassingly easy to dupe. They readily accepted his lies because they wanted to believe him. The years had finely honed his powers of persuasion, but he hadn't needed to work very hard convincing the business owners in Promise to trust him. Being born and raised in this very town had certainly helped. He nearly laughed out loud at how smoothly everything had gone.

Actually Richard did feel kind of bad about leaving a huge debt behind. Max Jordan was decent enough, even if he was an old fool. Billy from Billy D's was okay, too. One day—maybe—when he had money to spare, he'd consider paying everyone back. Grady and Savannah, too. That would shock his uptight brother.

It might all have worked if Richard could've persuaded Ellie Frasier to marry him. He experienced a twinge of regret. He must be losing his knack with women. Nothing could have shocked him more than Ellie's informing him she'd chosen Glen Patterson, instead.

Damn shame. Glen was a real hick, not all that different from Grady. Why Ellie would marry Glen when she could have had *him* was something he'd never understand. Women were fickle creatures, but until recently he'd been able to sway them to his way of thinking.

Not Ellie. How he would've loved to get his hands on her inheritance. That money would have gone a long way toward solving his problems. Well, it didn't do any good to cry over might-have-beens. He was a survivor and he'd prove it—not for the first time. Nothing kept Richard Weston down for long.

Calculating quickly, Richard figured he had only a few

days before everything went all to hell. He was ready. Grady seemed to think he idled away his days, but Richard had been working hard, preparing what he'd need. He'd been planning for this day almost from the moment he'd gotten back to Promise. Grady needn't worry; before long Richard would be out of his brother's hair.

Sure he had regrets. He'd thought about returning to Promise lots of times over the years, but he'd never suspected it would be for the reasons that had driven him here now.

When he'd first arrived on the ranch, he'd felt a faint stirring of emotion. It'd been a little less than six years since he'd set foot on the old homestead. Those feelings, however, hadn't lasted long and were completely dead now, especially since Grady had tossed him out of the house and forced him to sleep in the bunkhouse.

Richard couldn't grasp what it was that had kept his father and now his brother tied to a herd of four-footed headaches. He hated cattle, hated the way they smelled and bawled, the way they constantly needed care. Hated everything about them. This kind of life was never meant for him. Sadly no one appreciated that he was different. Better, if he did say so himself. Not even his mother had fully recognized it. Unfortunately neither did Savannah. Now that she'd married Laredo, she was even less inclined to side with him.

Sad to say, his time on the Yellow Rose was drawing to a close.

''Richard?''

Maggie Daniels peeked into the bunkhouse. The kid had become something of a pest lately, but he'd always been popular with children. They weren't all that different from women, most of them, eager for his attention.

''Howdy, cupcake,'' he said, forcing enthusiasm into his voice. ''Whatcha doin'?''

"Nothing. You want to play cards?"

"I can't now. How about later?" He leaned against the wall, clasping his hands behind his head.

"You said that last time." Her lower lip shot out.

Yup, kids were just like women; they pouted when they didn't get their way.

"Where's Savannah?" Richard asked, hoping to divert the kid's attention.

"In her garden."

"Didn't I hear her say something about baking cookies this afternoon?" He hadn't heard any such thing, but it'd get rid of the kid.

"She did?" Excitement tinged Maggie's voice.

"She told me so herself. Chocolate chip, my favorite. Why don't you ask her, and when you're finished you can bring me a sample. How does that sound?"

Maggie's eyes lit up and Richard laughed. He loved the fact that she preferred him over Grady. His big lug of a brother didn't know a damn thing about kids. It was comical watching him try to make friends with Maggie. She wouldn't have anything to do with him, and for once in his life Richard outshone his big brother.

"Come on, I'll go with you," he said, changing his mind. "We'll go talk to Savannah about those cookies."

"She's busy in her rose garden."

"But not too busy for us." Richard felt certain that was true. Savannah had a soft spot in her heart for the child and could refuse Maggie nothing. If he'd asked her on his own, chances were he wouldn't get to first base, but with Maggie holding his hand, Savannah was sure to capitulate.

For some reason Richard wanted one of those cookies. And he wanted it now.

He wasn't sure why—maybe just to pull Savannah's strings a bit. But Richard prided himself on getting what he wanted. Whenever he wanted it.

"YOU'RE FULL of surprises, Grady Weston," Caroline muttered to herself as she drove down the highway toward the Yellow Rose. The afternoon had dragged even though she'd been busy. Despite the heavy flow of traffic in and out of the post office, Caroline had frequently glanced at her watch, counting down the hours and then the minutes until closing time. And until she saw Grady again....

His invitation to lunch had caught her by surprise. She'd all but given up hope that he'd ever figure it out. In the past six months she'd done everything short of sending him a fax to let him know she was interested. When it came to romance, Grady Weston was as blind as they come. Not that she was any better; it'd taken her years to work up enough courage to give love a second chance.

She'd dated occasionally but never found that combination of mutual attraction and respect with anyone except Grady. Unfortunately she wasn't sure he recognized his own feelings, let alone hers. Twice now she'd decided to forget about him, and both times he'd given her reasons to believe it might work for them. Like showing up this afternoon and taking her to lunch.

She sped up, hoping their lunch date really *was* a beginning. She wanted a relationship with Grady, a romance—maybe even marriage eventually. Oh, my, but she did like him. He was honest, loyal, hardworking. She admired the way he'd struggled to hold on to the ranch despite grief and crippling sacrifices. Year after year she'd watched him do whatever it took to keep the Yellow Rose, to keep what was important to him and Savannah.

Caroline and Savannah had always been close, but never more so than now. Caroline's mother had died the year before, and it was Savannah who'd stood by her side and cried with her. Having buried her own mother, Savannah understood the grief that suffocated Caroline those first few months. It was also during that time that Maggie had grown so attached to Savannah, who'd become like a second mother to her. It pleased Caroline that her daughter loved Savannah as much as she did herself.

However, the five-year-old felt no such tenderness for Grady. Caroline sighed as her thoughts drifted to their rocky relationship. Grady's loud voice had made the child skittish from the first, and then one afternoon when Maggie was feeling ill, she'd phoned Savannah. Grady had answered the phone with a brusque demand, and from that moment forward Maggie would have nothing to do with him.

It was a problem, and one that continued to bother Caroline. If a romantic relationship developed between her and Grady the way she wanted, the way she dreamed, then Maggie and Grady would need to make their peace. True, Grady regretted the incident and had tried to undo the damage, but the child was unrelenting in her dislike of him.

As she reached the long gravel driveway leading to the Yellow Rose, Caroline decreased her speed to make the turn. A few moments later the large two-storey ranch house came into view. Rocket, Grady's old dog, lumbered stiffly down the porch steps to greet her, tail wagging.

Laredo was working in the corral while Savannah stood at the fence watching him put their prize stallion through his paces. Maggie was with Savannah, her feet braced against the bottom rail and her arms resting on top. When she heard the car, she leaped down and dashed toward her mother.

Maggie hurled herself into her arms as soon as Caroline stepped out of the car. ''Me and Savannah baked cookies!'' Her young voice rang with glee. ''And Richard said he never tasted better. He ate five cookies before he could stop himself.'' She slapped both hands over her mouth as though she'd blurted out a secret.

''How many did you eat?'' Caroline wanted to know. It

would be just like Richard to let the child spoil her dinner with cookies.

"Too many," Savannah answered for her, giving Caroline an apologetic half smile.

"We'll have a late dinner," Caroline said, dismissing her friend's worries. "I had a big lunch." She was about to tell Savannah about her lunch date when Grady burst out of the barn.

"Have you seen Richard? Has he shown up yet? He's got to be around here somewhere." Grady's face was distorted with rage.

Maggie edged closer to Caroline and wrapped her arm around her mother's waist.

"Grady," Savannah said in that low calming way of hers.

If Grady noticed Caroline, he gave no indication.

"Did I hear someone call for me?" Richard said, strolling out of the house as though he hadn't a care in the world. He was a handsome man, lean and muscular, probably the most attractive man Caroline had ever known. But, in Richard's case the good looks were superficial. She'd watched as he skillfully manipulated and used others to his own advantage. Even Grady and Savannah. She was amazed that Grady had allowed him to continue living on the ranch— yet at the same time, she understood. Like Savannah, Grady wanted to believe that Richard had changed.

Grady whirled around at the sound of Richard's voice. "We need to talk." His voice boomed and Maggie hid her face against Caroline's stomach.

"Max Jordan said he hasn't been paid," Grady shouted.

A shocked look stole over Richard. "You're joking! He didn't get the check? I put it in the mail two weeks ago."

"He never got it because you didn't mail it."

"What do you mean?" Richard demanded.

The two men faced off, Grady's anger spilling over in every word and Richard looking stunned and hard done by.

"Grady, please," Savannah said, hurrying toward her older brother and gently placing a hand on his arm. "Now isn't the time to be discussing this. Leave it until later."

"She's right," Richard said. "In case you hadn't noticed, we have company."

It was obvious that Grady had been so consumed by his anger, he'd barely realized they weren't alone. "Caroline," he murmured, and his face revealed both regret and delight. He seemed uncertain about what to say next. "Hello."

"How's my cupcake?" Richard asked, smiling at Maggie.

The little girl loosened her grip on Caroline's waist, turning to Richard as he spoke. He threw his arms open and she raced eagerly toward him.

"That's my girl," Richard said, catching Maggie and sweeping her high into the air. He whirled her around, the pair of them laughing as if it'd been days since they'd seen each other.

Savannah sidled closer to Caroline. "Grady's been looking for Richard all afternoon," she said in a quiet voice, "and he's been conveniently missing until now."

Caroline understood what her friend was saying. Richard had played his cards perfectly, appearing at the precise moment it'd be impossible for Grady to get a straight answer from him. Then he'd used Maggie's childish adoration to make Grady look even more foolish.

"Maggie," Caroline called.

Richard set the child back on her feet. Together the two of them joined Caroline and Savannah.

"I do believe Maggie has stolen my heart," he said, his eyes bright with laughter.

"Does that mean you'll marry me?" Maggie asked, grinning up at him.

"Sure thing."

"Really?"

"He won't marry you," Caroline said, reaching for her daughter's hand.

"Don't be so certain," Richard countered. He crouched down beside Maggie, but he was looking at Caroline.

"Hi, Maggie," Grady said, choosing that moment to try again. The anger had faded from his face, but he still held himself rigid.

Caroline gave him credit for making the effort to win Maggie over.

Her daughter wasn't easily swayed, however. She buried her face in Richard's shoulder.

"There's no need to be afraid of Grady," Richard whispered to Maggie—a stage whisper that carried easily. Then he smiled in a way that suggested Grady was wasting his time. In other words, Grady didn't have a snowball's chance in hell of convincing Maggie he wasn't an ogre. Richard's meaning couldn't have been clearer.

"I don't like Grady," Maggie announced, pursing her lips.

"Maggie!" Caroline admonished her.

"She's right, you know," Richard said, teeth flashing in a wide grin. "Grady just doesn't get along with kids, not like I do."

Caroline clamped her mouth shut rather than reveal her thoughts. She didn't trust Richard, *couldn't* trust him, not after the way he'd used his family. Used anyone who'd let him.

"I'm thinking Maggie needs someone like me in her life," Richard said. "Which means there's only one solution."

"What's that?" Caroline knew she was a fool to ask.

"You could always marry me," he said, and leaned over

far enough to touch his lips to Caroline's cheek. "Put me out of my misery, Caroline Daniels, and marry me."

"Oh, Mommy, let's do it!" Maggie shouted, clapping her hands. "Let's marry Richard."

Chapter Two

Grady was pleased that his sister had convinced Caroline and Maggie to stay for dinner. Now all he had to do was behave. It never seemed to fail—whenever he had a chance to make some headway with Maggie, he'd do something stupid. He wanted to blame Richard, but as usual he'd done it to himself.

His brother brought out the very worst in him. As Grady washed up for dinner, he hoped this evening would give him an opportunity to redeem himself in both Caroline and Maggie's eyes.

The table was already set and the food dished up in heaping portions. A platter of sliced roast beef rested in the middle, along with a huge bowl of mashed potatoes, a pitcher of gravy, fresh corn on the cob and a crisp green salad. There was also a basket filled with Savannah's mouthwatering buttermilk biscuits. His sister was one fine cook. He'd miss her when she moved into her own house with Laredo. But it was time, well past time, that she had a home and a life of her own. He knew from his talks with Laredo that they'd already started to think about adding to the family.

"Dinner looks wonderful," he said. Grady made an effort these days to let Savannah know how much he appreciated her. Over the years he'd taken her contributions for granted, discounting her efforts with her roses and her fledgling mail-order business—a business that now brought a significant income. He'd even made fun of her goats, which he considered pets rather than livestock. Now that she was married and about to establish her own home, Grady recognized just how much he was going to miss her.

Savannah flushed with pleasure at his praise.

The compliment had apparently earned him points with Caroline, too; she cast him an approving smile. Grady held in a sigh. He needed all the points he could get when it came to Caroline and Maggie. If everything went well, this evening might help him recapture lost ground with the child.

Everyone began to arrive for dinner. With the scent of the meal wafting through the house, it wasn't long before all the chairs were occupied—except for one. Richard's. It was just like his spoiled younger brother to keep everyone waiting.

"Where's Richard?" Maggie asked, glancing up at her mother.

Grady was asking himself the same question.

"He's coming, isn't he?" Maggie whined.

Even from where he stood Grady could sense the little girl's disappointment.

"I don't know, sweetheart," Caroline answered.

"There's no need to let our meal get cold," Grady said. If Richard chose to go without dinner, that was fine by him. If anything, he was grateful not to have his brother monopolizing the conversation, distracting both Caroline and Maggie. Grady pulled out his chair and sat down. Laredo, Savannah and Caroline did so, as well. The only one who remained standing was Maggie.

"What about Richard?" she asked in a small stubborn voice.

"I guess he isn't hungry," Caroline said, and pulled out the chair next to her own for Maggie.

"He promised he'd sit next to me at dinner."

"It isn't a good idea to believe in the things Richard promises," Grady said as much for Caroline's ears as for her daughter's. He hated to disappoint the five-year-old, but it was God's own truth. Richard was about as stable as beef prices. His loyalties constantly shifted toward whatever was most advantageous to him, with little concern for anyone else.

His playful marriage proposal to Caroline worried Grady. She'd laughed it off, but Grady found no humor in it. Apparently his brother knew Grady was interested in Caroline and thus considered her fair game. It would be typical of Richard to do what he could to thwart any romance between Caroline and Grady by making a play for her himself. Grady knew that made him sound paranoid, but he thought his fears were justified. Experience had been an excellent teacher.

He reached for the meat and forked a thick slice of roast beef onto his plate, then passed the platter to Caroline.

Maggie folded her arms and stared defiantly at Grady. "I'm not eating until Richard's here."

"Maggie, please," Caroline cajoled. She glanced at Grady, her eyes apologetic.

"Grady yelled at Richard."

Once again Grady was the culprit. "I shouldn't have yelled, should I?" He was careful to speak in a low quiet voice. "I do that sometimes without thinking, but I wasn't angry at you."

"You were mad at Richard."

No use lying about it. "Yes, I was."

"And now he won't come to dinner."

"I think Richard has other reasons for not showing up," Caroline explained as she placed a scoop of mashed potatoes on her daughter's plate. "Do you want one of Savannah's yummy buttermilk biscuits?"

Maggie hesitated for a long moment before she shook her head. "I won't eat without Richard."

"Did I hear someone call my name?" Richard asked cheerfully as he stepped into the kitchen. "Sorry I'm late," he said, not sounding the least apologetic. He pulled out his chair, sat down beside Maggie and reached for the meat platter all in a single graceful movement.

Caroline's child shot Grady a triumphant look as if to say she'd known all along that Richard hadn't lied to her.

Grady's appetite vanished. For every step he advanced in his effort to make friends with Maggie, he seemed to retreat two. Once more Richard had made him look like a fool in front of the little girl. And once more he'd allowed it to happen.

"Is it true you want to marry my mom?" Maggie asked Richard with such hopefulness that the question silenced all other conversation.

"Of course it's true." Richard chuckled, then winked at Caroline.

"I think you should," Maggie said, hanging on Richard's every word.

Grady didn't speak again during the entire meal. Not that anyone noticed. Adored by Maggie, Richard was in his element, and he became the center of attention, joking and teasing, complimenting Savannah, even exchanging a brief joke with Laredo.

Caroline was quiet for a time, but soon, Grady noted, Richard had won her over just as he had everyone else. Despite his disappointment, Grady marveled at his brother's talent. Richard had always savored attention, whereas Grady avoided the limelight. It had never bothered him before, but now he felt a growing resentment, certain Caroline was about to be caught by the force of Richard's spell. Other than Ellie Fraiser, Grady had never known any woman to resist his brother's charms. Ellie was the exception, and only because she was already in love with Glen Patterson, although neither of them had recognized the strength of their feelings for each other—until Richard interfered. Indirectly, and definitely without intending it, Richard had brought about something good. Still, if it hadn't been for Glen in Ellie's life, Grady wondered what would have happened. That, at least, was one worry he'd escaped.

As soon as he could, Grady excused himself from the table and headed toward the barn. He would have liked to linger over dinner, perhaps enjoy a cup of coffee with Caroline on the porch, but he could see that was a lost cause.

Not until he'd stalked across the yard did he recognize the symptoms. Damn it all, he was *jealous*. The only woman he'd ever cared about, and Richard was going to steal her away. The problem was, Grady had no idea how to keep him from Caroline.

To his surprise Laredo followed him outside. Like Grady, his brother-in-law was a man of few words.

"Don't let him get to you," Laredo said, leading the way into the barn.

"I'm not," Grady told him, which wasn't entirely a lie. He knew the kind of man Richard was; he knew the insecurity of Richard's charm. He didn't like the fact that his brother was working on Caroline, but he wasn't willing to make a fool of himself, either. Other men had made that mistake before him. Glen Patterson, for one. The poor guy had come off looking like an idiot at the Cattlemen's Association dance. Richard and Glen had nearly come to blows over Ellie, with half the town looking on. They might have, too, if Sheriff Hennessey hadn't stepped in when he did.

"Good." Laredo slapped him on the back and the two went their separate ways.

Grady didn't stay in the barn long. He gave himself ample time to control his resentment, then decided that, while he wasn't going to accept the role of fool, he didn't intend to just give up, either. He'd tried to make sure Caroline understood that their lunch today was more than a meal between friends. Hell—despite what she'd said—he didn't know if she ever considered him a friend.

Grady found her sitting on the porch with Savannah sipping hot tea. Maggie sat on the steps cradling her doll. He strolled toward the women, without a clue what to say once he joined them. He supposed he'd better learn a few conversational rules, he thought grimly, if that meant he'd have a chance with Caroline.

The two women stopped talking as he approached, which led him to surmise that he'd been the topic of conversation. He felt as awkward as a schoolboy and, not sure what else to do, touched the rim of his hat.

Savannah, bless her heart, winked conspiratorially at him and stood. "Maggie," she said, holding out her hand to the little girl, "I found one of my old dolls this afternoon. Would you like to play with her?"

Maggie leaped to her feet. "Could I?"

"You bet."

As Savannah and Maggie disappeared into the house, Grady lowered himself onto the rocker his sister had vacated. He felt as tongue-tied and unsure as he had that afternoon. Taking a deep breath, he forced himself to remember that he'd been talking to Caroline all her life. It shouldn't be any different now.

"Beautiful night, isn't it?" he commented, thinking the weather was a safe subject with which to start.

"Those look like storm clouds to the east."

Grady hadn't noticed. He gazed up at the sky, feeling

abashed, until Caroline leaned back in her rocker and laughed. He grinned, loving the sound of her amusement. It was difficult not to stare. All these years, and he hadn't seen how damn beautiful she was. While he could speculate why it'd taken him this long, he didn't want to waste another minute. It was all he could do to keep his tongue from lolling out the side of his mouth whenever he caught sight of her. He longed to find the words to tell her how attractive she was, how much he liked and respected her. It wasn't the first time he'd wished he could issue compliments with Richard's finesse.

"Come on, Grady, loosen up."

"I'm loose," he growled, and noted how relaxed she was, rocking back and forth as if they often sat side by side in the evening. His parents had done that. Every night. They'd shared the events of their day, talked over plans for the future, exchanged feelings and opinions.

The memory of his mother and father filled his mind. Six years, and the pain of their absence was as strong now as it had been in the beginning. Some nights Grady would sit on the porch, the old dog beside him, and silently discuss business matters with his father, seeking his advice. Not that he actually expected his father to provide answers, of course; Grady was no believer in ghosts or paranormal influences. But those one-sided discussions had helped see Grady through the rough years. It was during those times, burdened with worries, that he'd been forced to search deep inside himself for the answers. And on rare occasions, he'd experienced moments when he'd felt his father's presence more intensely than his absence.

"You've gotten quiet all of a sudden," Caroline said.

"I want to talk to you about Richard." His words were as much a surprise to him as to Caroline.

"Oh?" Her eyebrows rose.

"I realize you must find his attention flattering, but like

I said earlier it isn't wise to believe anything Richard says.'' The lazy sway of her rocking stopped. ''I know you probably don't want to hear this,'' he added. It wasn't pleasant for him, either. Regardless of anything between them, though, Grady's one concern was that Richard not hurt Caroline.

''I appreciate what you're doing, but I'm a big girl.''

''I didn't mean to suggest you weren't. It's just that, well, Richard has a way with women.''

''And you assume he's going to sweep me off my feet, is that it?'' The teasing warmth in her voice was gone, replaced by something less friendly.

''You think I want to say these things?'' he asked, inhaling sharply. ''It isn't really you he's interested in, anyway.''

''I beg your pardon?''

Grady wished he'd never introduced the subject. Clearly Caroline wasn't going to appreciate his insight, but once he'd started he couldn't stop. ''Richard knows how I feel about you and—'' He snapped his mouth closed before he embarrassed himself further. ''I'm only telling you this because I don't want you to get hurt again.'' He didn't know what madness possessed him to add the *again*. He realized the moment he did that Caroline had taken his advice the wrong way.

Grady had never asked her about Maggie's father, didn't intend to do so now. Heaven knew she was touchy enough about the subject. The only other time he'd said something, months earlier, she'd been ready to bite his head off.

''This discussion is over,'' she said, jumping to her feet.

''Caroline, I didn't mean— Oh, hell, be angry if you want.'' With an abrupt movement, he got out of the chair, leaving it to rock wildly. Once again he'd botched their conversation. ''It appears you don't need any advice from me.''

''No, Grady, I don't.''

It damaged his pride that she'd so casually disregard his warning. ''Fine, then, for all I care, you can marry Richard.'' Not giving her a chance to respond, he stalked away, absolutely certain that any hope of a relationship was forever ruined.

His fears were confirmed less than an hour later when he left the barn and saw her again. She was in her car with the driver's window rolled down. Richard was leaning against the side of the vehicle, and the sound of their laughter rang in the twilight.

The unexpected twist of disappointment and pain caught Grady off guard. Well, that certainly answered that.

Caroline must have noticed him because Richard suddenly looked over his shoulder. Grady didn't stick around. It was too hard to pretend he didn't care when he damn well did. His stride was full of purpose as he crossed the yard and stormed into the house, sequestering himself in the office.

His emotions had covered the full range in a single day. He'd taken Caroline to lunch and afterward felt…ecstatic; there was no other word for it. Before dinner he'd been like a kid, thrilled to see her again so soon. Now, just a few hours later, he'd been thrown into despair, convinced beyond doubt that he'd lost whatever chance he might have had with her.

It was enough to drive a man to drink. He sat in the worn leather desk chair and pulled open the bottom file drawer. His father had kept a bottle of bourbon there for times when nothing else would do, and Grady had followed the same practice. The bottle was gone—which had happened before. Grady suspected Richard, with good reason, but at the moment he didn't really care. He wasn't much of a drinking man. A cold beer now and then suited him just fine, but he'd never enjoyed the hard stuff.

The knock on the office door surprised him. "Who is it?" he barked, not in the mood for company.

"Richard." His brother didn't wait for an invitation but opened the door and sauntered in. He immediately made himself at home, claiming the only other chair in the room. He leaned back, locked his fingers behind his head and grinned like a silly schoolboy.

"So what's up with you and Caroline?" he asked.

Grady scowled. The last person he wanted to discuss with his brother was Caroline. "Nothing."

His denial only served to fuel Richard's amusement. "Come on, Grady, I've got eyes in my head. It's obvious you've got the hots for her. Not that I blame you, man. She's one nice-looking woman."

Grady didn't like Richard's tone of voice, but prolonging this conversation by arguing with him would serve no useful purpose. "Listen, Richard, I've got better things to do than sit around discussing Caroline Daniels with you."

"I don't imagine it would take much to talk her into the sack, either. She's already been to bed with at least one man—what's a few more? Right?"

Grady ground his teeth in an effort to control his irritation. "I don't think it's a good idea for us to discuss Caroline." He stood and walked over to the door and pointedly opened it.

"I wouldn't mind getting into her bed myself one of these days," Richard went on.

Despite everything he'd promised himself, Grady saw red. He flew across the room and dragged his brother out of the chair, grabbing him by the front of his shirt.

Richard held up both hands. "Hey, hey, don't get so riled! I was only teasing."

Grady's fingers ached with the strength of his grip. It took a moment to clear his head enough to release his brother.

"You don't want to talk about Caroline, fine," Richard said, backing toward the door. "But you can't blame a guy for asking, can you?"

DRIVING HOME, Caroline realized she not only distrusted Richard Weston, but thoroughly disliked him. Before she'd left the Yellow Rose, he'd gone out of his way to let her know that Grady had asked Nell Bishop, a local widow, to the Cattlemen's dance earlier in the summer. What was particularly meaningful about the information was that Caroline knew how hard Savannah had tried to convince Grady to invite *her*. He almost had. She remembered he'd come into the post office a few days before the dance, but within minutes they'd ended up trading insults. That was unfortunate. He *had* mentioned the dance, though, leaving her to wonder.

Their verbal exchanges were legendary. Only in the past couple of weeks had they grown comfortable enough with each other to manage a civil conversation.

Now this.

Caroline didn't believe Richard. She strongly suspected that almost everything out of his mouth was a lie. If the story about Nell *was* true, she would've heard about it. To the best of her knowledge Nell hadn't even attended the dance. Not that it was unusual for her to avoid social functions—it was widely known that Nell continued to grieve for Jake, the only man she'd ever loved. He'd been her high-school sweetheart, and their affection for each other had been evident throughout the years. Caroline had often wondered if Nell would remarry.

"Ask her." Caroline spoke the words aloud without realizing it.

"Ask who, Mommy?" Maggie looked at her mother.

"A friend." She left it at that.

"About what?"

"Nothing." She smiled at her daughter and changed the subject.

As it turned out she had the opportunity to chat with Nell sooner than she'd expected. The following afternoon on her way home from work Caroline stopped at the local Winn-Dixie for a few groceries.

She collected what she needed and pushed her cart up to the checkout stand—behind Nell.

"Howdy, friend," Nell said cheerfully. "Haven't seen you in awhile."

"Nell!" Caroline didn't disguise her pleasure. "How are you?"

"Great. I've been working hard on getting the word out that I'm turning Twin Canyons into a dude ranch. The brochures were mailed to travel agents last week."

Caroline admired her ingenuity. "That's terrific."

The grocery clerk slid Nell's purchases over the scanner, coming up with the total. She paid in cash, then glanced around. "Jeremy!" she called. "Emma." She reached for the plastic bags, giving a good-natured shrug. "I warned those two not to wander off. I know exactly where to find them, too—the book section. They're both crazy about books, especially the Babysitters' Club books and that new series of kids' Westerns by T. R. Grant. I can't buy them fast enough."

Caroline recognized both series. T. R. Grant was the current rage; even Maggie had wanted Caroline to read her his books. Maggie was still a bit young for them, but it wouldn't be long before she devoured Grant's books and the Babysitters' Club by herself.

"Have you got a moment?" Caroline asked, opening her purse to pay for her own groceries.

"Sure." Nell waited while Caroline finished her transaction. "What can I do for you?"

As they walked toward the book display at the far end

of the Winn-Dixie, Caroline mulled over the best way to approach the subject of Nell and Grady. She wasn't sure why she'd allowed Richard to upset her, especially when she believed it'd all been a lie. Not that she'd blame Grady for being attracted to Nell. In fact, at one time she'd believed they might eventually marry. They seemed right together somehow; both were ranchers and both had struggled against what seemed impossible odds.

In the back of her mind Caroline had always suspected that when the time was right, they'd discover each other. Grady and Jake had been good friends, and Grady had been a pall bearer at Jake's funeral. Grady and Nell were close in age and would make a handsome couple. Grady was an inch or two over six feet, with a broad muscular physique not unlike Jake's. There weren't many men who'd suit Nell physically, since she was nearly six feet herself.

"I hope you don't think I'm being nosy, but I heard a rumor…" Caroline blurted before she lost her nerve. This was even more embarrassing than she'd feared.

"About what?" Nell frowned.

Caroline drew a breath and held it until her lungs ached. "About you and Grady Weston."

Nell frowned again. "Me and Grady?"

Caroline nodded.

"Grady's a friend," Nell said. "I've always liked him and if I were ever to consider remarrying, I'd certainly think about Grady."

Caroline broke eye contact. This wasn't what she'd wanted to hear.

"He's a good man and he'd make an excellent husband and father," Nell continued, then asked a probing question of her own. "Is there any reason you're asking?"

"Not really."

"He asked me to the dance last month," Nell added, as if she'd suddenly remembered.

So it was true. Caroline's spirits sank.

"In fact, I received two invitations to the dance within a few hours." This was said with a note of amusement.

"Two? Grady and who else?"

Nell's mouth widened in a smile. "You aren't going to believe this, but both Grady Weston and Glen Patterson asked me to the dance."

"Glen?" That was a kicker, considering he was now engaged to Ellie Frasier. Those two were so deeply in love it was difficult to imagine that little more than a month ago Glen had invited Nell and not Ellie to the biggest dance of the year. In the end he'd gone by himself and then he'd practically come to blows with Richard over Ellie. Richard—always the spoiler.

"I don't know what was in the air that day," Nell murmured. "Grady and Glen calling me up like that."

"Did you go to the dance?"

"Briefly," Nell said, "but Emma had an upset stomach that day. I made an appearance, said hello to some friends I don't see often and left shortly after the music started."

"Grady was there," Caroline said, fondly recalling their one dance. Ladies' choice, and she'd been the one to approach him. Those few short minutes in Grady's arms had been wonderful. Afterward she'd hoped he'd ask her to dance himself, but he'd wandered back to where he'd been sitting with Cal Patterson and hadn't spoken to her again. Caroline had felt bitterly disappointed.

"...any reason?" Nell asked.

Caroline caught only the last part of the question. "Reason?" she repeated.

"That you're asking about me and Grady?"

"Not really," she said, then figured she owed her friend the truth. "He asked me to lunch the other day."

"And you went?"

Caroline nodded.

"And you had a good time?"

"A great time," Caroline admitted.

Nell shifted the weight of the groceries in her hands. "Listen, Caroline, if you're worried about there being anything romantic between me and Grady, don't give it another thought. Grady's one of the most honorable men I know, but—" her voice dipped with emotion "—I'm still in love with Jake."

"Oh, Nell." Caroline hugged her friend.

"Oh, damn it all," Nell said, blinking furiously. "I've got to scoot. I'll see you soon, okay?"

"Sure." It would be good to sit down and talk with her friend. Both their lives were so busy it was difficult to find the time.

"Jeremy. Emma." Nell called her children again, and the two came running.

Caroline waved them off and headed toward the parking lot, deep in thought. So, what Richard had told her was true. This was what made him dangerous. He tossed in a truth now and then just to keep everyone guessing. But for once, she wished he'd been lying.

GRADY HAD BEEN PENSIVE ever since the night Caroline stayed for dinner, Savannah observed. He sat at the kitchen table, supposedly writing out an order for Richard to pick up at the feed store later that afternoon. But for the last five minutes, all he'd done was stare blankly into space.

Savannah had to bite her tongue. Laredo had repeatedly warned her against any further matchmaking efforts between her brother and Caroline, but he might as well have asked her to stop breathing. Grady was miserable and Caroline hadn't been any happier. If it was within her power to bring them together—these two people who were so obviously meant for each other—what possible harm could it do?

Considering that thought, Savannah poured her brother a fresh cup of coffee.

Grady glanced up and thanked her with an off-center smile.

"Something on your mind?" she asked. If he voluntarily brought up the subject, all the better.

"Nothing important," he murmured, and reached for the steaming mug. He raised it tentatively to his lips, then glanced at her as if tempted to seek her advice.

Savannah held her breath, hoping Grady would ask her about Caroline. He didn't.

"The church dinner's this weekend," she said, speaking quickly.

Grady responded with what sounded like a grunt, the translation of which she already knew. He wasn't interested.

Savannah glared at him. If she wrung his neck, she wondered, would he have any idea why? "Caroline's bringing her applesauce cake," she added casually. "Her mother's recipe."

At the mention of her friend's name, Grady raised his head. "Caroline's going to the church dinner?"

"Of course." At last, a reaction. Her brother might be one of the most intelligent men she knew, but when it came to women he was the class dunce. "I'm bringing my chicken teriyaki salad,'' she added, as if this was significant.

''Is Laredo going?''

''Yes, and Ellie and Glen and just about everyone else in town.''

''Oh.''

Savannah figured she was due a large heavenly reward for her patience. *Oh.* Was that all he could say? Poor Caroline.

''It isn't a date thing, is it?''

Savannah didn't know how to answer. If she let him assume everyone was bringing a date, it might scare him off. On the other hand, if she said nothing, someone else might ask Caroline.

''This shouldn't be such a difficult question,'' Grady said, glaring at her.

''Yes and no. Some people will come with dates and some won't.''

He mulled that over. ''Does Caroline have a date?''

Savannah had to restrain herself from hugging Grady's neck and crying out for joy. He wasn't as dense as she'd thought. ''Not that I know of.'' This, too, was said casually, as though she hadn't the least bit of interest in Caroline's social life.

''Oh.''

Grady was back to testing her patience again. She waited an entire minute before she ventured another question.

''Are you thinking of inviting her and Maggie?''

''Me?'' Grady's eyes widened as if this were a new thought.

''Yes, you,'' she returned pointedly.

"I'm...thinking about it," he finally said.

Her face broke out in a smile and she clapped her hands. "That's wonderful."

"What's wonderful?" Richard asked, wandering into the kitchen. He reached for a banana, peeled it and leaned expectantly against the kitchen counter.

Grady and Savannah exchanged looks. "The church dinner," she answered for them both.

"Yeah, I heard about that," he said with his mouth full. "Either of you going?"

"I think so." Again Savannah took the initiative.

"Then I'll give some thought to attending, too."

Both Grady and Savannah remained silent.

"I should probably have a date, though, don't you think?" He pondered his own question. "Caroline. I'll ask Caroline," he said triumphantly. "She'll jump at the chance to go with me."

Chapter Three

"You're a damn fool, that's what you are," Grady muttered as he barreled down the highway toward Promise, driving twenty miles over the speed limit.

The reason for this hasty trip had to do with Caroline Daniels. By dinnertime he'd recognized that either he made his move now and invited her to the church dinner or let Richard beat him to the punch. Of course he could have just phoned and been done with it, but that didn't seem right, not when anyone on the ranch could pick up a telephone receiver and listen in on the conversation. By anyone, he meant Richard. Besides, Grady preferred to talk to Caroline in person; it seemed more...meaningful.

He'd never been good at this courtship thing, but damn it all, he wasn't going to let his brother cheat him out of taking Caroline and Maggie to that church dinner. Richard wasn't interested in Caroline—Grady was sure of it—any more than he'd fallen head over heels in love with Ellie Frasier. His brother was far more concerned with cheating him out of the pleasure of Caroline's company. Except that he had no intention of standing idly by and letting it happen.

Once he'd made his decision, Grady knew he should act on it. Naturally there was always the risk that he'd arrive at Caroline's with his heart dangling from his sleeve only to learn that Richard had already asked her out for Saturday night.

Even knowing he might be too late didn't stop him. He wanted to attend the dinner with Caroline and Maggie more than he'd wanted anything in a long while. It surprised him how much.

The drive into town, during which he thought about the approach he'd take with Caroline, seemed to take no time at all. His goal was to ask her to be his date before Richard did, and at the same time keep his pride intact if she refused. No small task, considering past experience.

He parked in front of Caroline's small house and leaped out of the truck cab. Eager to get this settled, he took the steps up to her front door two at a time and leaned on the buzzer.

Caroline opened the door, her face registering surprise.

"Grady, hello." She recovered quickly and held the screen door wide.

"Would you like to sit outside for a spell?" he asked, instead gesturing toward the porch swing. Since he was nervous about this entire thing, staying outside in the semi-darkness felt more inviting than her well-lit living room.

"Sure."

She glanced over her shoulder, and Grady noticed Maggie playing by herself in the background. She had her dolls sitting around a small table and was chatting amicably as she stood in front of her play kitchen cooking up a storm. He grinned at the sight.

Caroline sat down, but Grady found it impossible to keep still.

"Did Savannah phone?" he asked. It would be just like his sister to give Caroline a heads-up. He hadn't announced where he was going when he left the ranch, but Savannah knew. After all, she was the one who'd steered him in this direction in that less-than-subtle way of hers. Grady tolerated Savannah's matchmaking only because he wasn't opposed to her efforts to promote a romance between him and Caroline. Frankly he could use the help. He wasn't keen, however, on letting her know that.

"Savannah phone me?" Caroline repeated. "No, she hasn't."

Grady released a sigh, and some of the tension eased from between his shoulder blades. "What about Richard?"

"What about him?"

"Have you spoken to him recently—say, in the last four or five hours?"

"No," she answered curtly. "Is there a reason for all these questions?"

Grady could see that Caroline was growing impatient but he needed the answers to both questions before he could proceed. "Of course there's a reason," he snapped, annoyed with his lack of finesse when it came to romance. "I don't want to end up looking ridiculous, thanks to Richard."

"What's Richard got to do with anything?" Caroline demanded.

"If he's been here first, just say so and I'll be on my way." The thought of Richard and Caroline together did funny things to his stomach. He'd never been a jealous man; it was an unfamiliar—and unpleasant—sensation. But he wasn't about to let Richard walk all over him.

"It seems to me, Grady, that you don't need Richard in order to look ridiculous. You do a damn good job all by yourself!"

Her words took him by surprise. He exhaled, counting to ten, in an effort to calm his racing heart, then leaned against the porch railing and faced her. "All I want to know is if Richard already asked you to the church dinner."

Her eyes briefly widened when she understood the reason

for his unexpected visit. Caroline smiled slowly and sweetly. It was a smile he'd seen all too rarely from her. He found it difficult to look away.

"Why do you want to know?" she asked.

"I told you already," he blurted out. "If Richard's already asked you, then I'll save my breath."

"What if I said he hasn't asked me? Does that mean you will?"

His pride was a fierce thing and had gotten him into trouble with her in the past. He tucked his hands in his back pockets, shrugging as if it was of little concern. "I might."

Caroline set the swing in motion and relaxed enough to cross her legs. She was wearing shorts, and the movement granted him the opportunity to admire those legs.

"Let me put it like this," Caroline said after a moment. "If Richard *had* asked me, and I'm not saying he has, I'd turn him down."

"You would?" This gave Grady second thoughts. If she'd turn down his brother, there was nothing to say she wouldn't do the same with him. "What about me?" he asked before considering the question.

"But you haven't asked me," she reminded him.

If she was leading him on a merry chase, he swore he'd never forgive her. "Will you…would you and Maggie be my date for the church dinner Saturday night?"

The joy that lit her eyes was all the answer Grady needed. His heart felt as if it might fly straight out of his chest.

"We'd love to go with you," Caroline answered without hesitation.

"That'd be great. Great!" He started to leave, but caught the toe of his boot on a toy Maggie had left on the porch and damn near fell on his face. Not that it would have mattered. He was too damn happy to let a minor humiliation detract from his pleasure.

He was halfway to his truck when Caroline stopped him. "Do you want me to meet you at the church?" she called out.

"No." What kind of date did she think this was, anyway? "I'll pick you both up." Just so there was no room for misunderstanding, he added, "This is a date, Caroline."

"Any particular time?"

Details. Leave it to a woman to be concerned about something like that. "When do you want me?"

"Six-forty-five sounds about right."

"Then that's when I'll be here."

She walked to the porch steps and wrapped her arm around the white column. "I'll look forward to seeing you Saturday."

It would have been the most natural thing in the world to jump up and shout, he was that happy. Happy enough to feel almost drunk with it. Damn it all, he hadn't even kissed Caroline yet. If he got giddy from a little thing like this, he could only begin to imagine what it would be like the first time they made love.

REVEREND WADE MCMILLEN liked nothing better than social gatherings at the church, and this one was special, celebrating the one hundred and twentieth anniversary of the date Promise Christian Church had been established. He'd been ministering to this small but growing flock for five years now. It was his first assignment, and friends in the ministry had told him there was something special about a minister's first church. This had certainly proved to be the case with Wade. The parishioners who crowded the church hall were as much his family as the people he'd left behind.

Raised in Houston, Wade had been around cattle ranchers and oil men from the time he was old enough to pull on a pair of cowboy boots. No one was more surprised when he was called to the ministry than Wade himself. His experience in Promise had shown him that he loved his work more than any other occupation he might have chosen.

Long tables at the far end of the hall were heaped with a variety of some of the best home cooking in Texas. Main courses, salads, desserts. Once the food had been readied, Wade led the assembled families in grace, then stayed out of the way while the women's group got the buffet lines going. His role in all this was to make sure dinner went smoothly and everyone had what he or she needed.

"In my opinion," Louise Powell said, pulling Wade aside, "Savannah Smith's teriyaki salad with *chicken* should be considered a main course and not a salad. It's misleading for those of us who're watching our weight to be tempted with salads that under normal circumstances would be considered a main course."

Louise and her friend Tammy Lee Kollenborn had been a trial to Wade from the start, but he wasn't alone in his struggles with these two women. Heaven help him if he inadvertently crossed either of them.

"I'm afraid I'm the one to blame for that," Wade explained, attempting to sound apologetic. "Savannah put it on the table with the main courses, and I suggested that since it was technically a salad, it belonged there."

"I see," Louise said, and tightly pinched her lips together, letting him know she disapproved.

"I'll make sure I don't make that mistake again," he said. "Perhaps next year you'd volunteer to help the women's group set up the hall. I'm sure they'd appreciate your advice on such important matters as what should and shouldn't be considered a salad."

"I'll do that," she said with a tinge of self-righteousness.

She patted his hand and excused herself to return to her husband.

The buffet line had dwindled down to only a few stragglers, and rather than become embroiled in any more culinary controversies, Wade reached for a plate and a set of silverware, then stepped to the end of the line.

He scanned the group, looking for an empty seat. The circular tables seated eight, perfect for accommodating four couples. The Royal Heirs, the seniors' social group, occupied four of those tables. No space there.

Ellie Frasier and Glen Patterson sat in a corner of the large bustling hall with their friends. There were a few empty spaces, but their table would fill up soon. He enjoyed Ellie and Glen and was counseling them before their wedding. They'd been in for three sessions now, and he had a strong feeling they were well suited. Their marriage would be a good one, built on a foundation of friendship.

Savannah and Laredo Smith were sitting next to Ellie and Glen. Now, there were two he'd never suspected would be right for each other. Savannah was a gentle soul, a special woman who'd touched his heart. Laredo had drifted into town; somehow he and Savannah had been drawn together. Love had changed them both, Savannah especially. Looking at them now, just a short time after their wedding, it was difficult to remember that they'd been together only months rather than years.

Frank Hennessey, the town sheriff, got in line behind Wade. "This is a great spread, isn't it, Rev?"

"As I've said more than once," Wade reminded the other man, "Promise Christian has some of the best cooks in the state of Texas."

"Amen to that." Frank handed Dovie Boyd a plate before reaching for one himself. Both close to retirement age, the two had been seeing each other for as long as Wade had served the community, but apparently didn't have plans to marry. Wade had never questioned them about their relationship. That was their business, not his. He was fond of Frank and Dovie. He found their company delightful and was happy to let Dovie spoil him with a home-cooked meal every now and then. The woman was a wonder with apple pie.

One of Nell Bishop's children raced across the room, and Wade's spirits lifted. He'd sit with Nell, he decided. The widow might feel like odd man out, being there without a date, and since he was alone himself, well, it would work nicely. Nell was a safe dinner companion; everyone knew she wasn't interested in remarriage. If Wade chose to dine with one of the single ladies, some women in the congregation, Louise Powell and Tammy Lee Kollenborn in particular, were sure to read it as a sign of incipient romance.

So Nell was the perfect choice. No pressures there. Not only that, he had a great deal of respect and affection for her family. He'd enjoy spending the evening with them.

But Nell was sitting with her mother-in-law and their table was full.

Wade had to admit he felt lonely. Everyone present seemed to be part of a couple, and those who were single had found partners. Even Grady Weston had a date, and frankly, Wade was pleased with his choice. He'd long admired Caroline Daniels; she and Grady seemed right together, a thought that had occurred to him more than once since Savannah's wedding.

Not until Wade was at the end of the dessert table did he spot the ideal location. He smiled, amused that the vacant seat was at the very table he'd considered moments earlier. The empty spot was next to Cal Patterson. Wade got along just fine with the rancher, although the man had a reputation for being prickly. Cal sat with his brother Glen, but Glen wasn't paying him any heed. The younger Patterson's concentration was held by Ellie, and rightly so.

"Mind if I join you?" Wade asked Cal.

"Mind?" Cal muttered, sliding his chair over to give Wade ample room. "I'd be grateful."

"This is a great way to celebrate the church's birthday, isn't it?" Wade asked, digging into his food with gusto. He never ate better than at church dinners.

"Growing up, I can remember looking forward to the third Saturday in July," Cal said. "My mom made her special baked beans every year. Still does. Apparently the recipe's been handed down from one generation to the next for at least a hundred years. If I remember right, it originally came from back East."

Wade took a forkful of the baked beans and nodded approvingly. "Mmm." He chewed slowly, savoring every morsel. "There's a lot to be said for tradition, especially when it tastes this good."

"She only bakes 'em once a year and it's always for the church." Having cleaned his own plate, Cal pushed back his chair and folded his arms. Wade's gaze followed Cal's. Grady and Caroline stood in the dessert line with Savannah and Laredo. The four were engaged in conversation and appeared to be enjoying themselves.

"Grady and Caroline make a handsome couple, don't they?" Wade asked, testing the waters with the older Patterson brother. This couldn't be easy on him, especially after Cal's own unfortunate experience a few years earlier. His wedding had been canceled just two days before the ceremony. Cal had taken the brunt of the embarrassment when his fiancée abruptly left town.

Wade and Cal had shared some serious discussions afterward and bonded as friends. But Cal hadn't mentioned Jennifer's name, not in all the time since. The subject of marriage appeared to be taboo, as well. More than once Wade had been tempted to remind Cal not to judge all women by Jennifer's actions. It might be a cliché, but time really was a great healer. When Cal was ready, Wade believed he'd date again.

"It's about time Grady opened his eyes," Cal said, grinning.

"About Caroline?"

"Yeah. Those two have been circling each other for a year, maybe more. If one of 'em didn't make a move soon, I was going to rope 'em together myself."

Wade chuckled, enjoying the image.

"Seems that every time Grady gets close to making a move, something happens and he takes off like a jackrabbit."

Little Maggie Daniels raced past at that moment, and Wade caught her about the waist to keep her from colliding with Nell Bishop's son. "Whoa there," he said, laughing. "What's the big hurry?"

Maggie covered her mouth and giggled. "Petey was chasing me."

"Be careful, understand?"

Maggie bobbed her head, and Wade pointed to the corsage on her wrist. "Who gave you flowers?"

"Grady," Maggie answered with such pride her entire face lit up. Her eyes fell to the pink and white carnations on her wrist. "He yells sometimes."

"Does it bother you?"

Maggie had to think about that a moment before she shrugged. "He bought Mommy flowers, too. She was surprised and so was I, and when Mommy asked him why, he said it was 'cause we're special."

"You are very special." Wade smiled.

Maggie's return smile revealed two missing front teeth. "Mommy likes him," she said, and Wade had the feeling that she'd decided perhaps Grady wasn't such a bad guy, after all.

Petey Bush approached. "Wanna hold hands?" the six-year-old boy asked.

Maggie looked to Wade for permission. "I think it'll be all right," he advised.

She nodded solemnly and the two children strolled off hand in hand.

"It's a sorry day when five- and six-year-olds have an easier time getting a date than we do, don't you think?" Cal asked him.

A sorry day indeed, Wade mused.

CAROLINE HAD a wonderful time at the dinner. A *perfectly* wonderful time, she reflected as they walked out to Grady's truck. Everything about the evening had been like a dream. Not once had she exchanged a cross word with Grady. Not once had they disagreed. Not once had he yelled at Maggie. There just might be hope for them.

Maggie, worn-out from the evening's activities, fell asleep between them in the truck. She slumped against Caroline, her head in her mother's lap. When Grady pulled up in front of the house, she was still asleep. It seemed a shame to disturb her.

Grady must have thought the same thing, because he turned off the engine and made no move to get out of the truck. The only light available was from a quarter moon set crookedly in the dark Texas sky.

Night settled about them. Neither one of them spoke. For her own part, Caroline wanted the evening to last as long as possible. If it never ended, that was fine with her.

"I had a lovely time," she finally whispered.

"Me, too."

She assumed he'd open the truck door then and was pleased when he didn't.

"It was sweet of you to bring Maggie and me flowers."

"It was the only way I could tell you how much—" He halted midsentence.

"How much…?" she prodded.

"I like you both," he finished.

"Do you, Grady?" she asked, her voice low.

"Very much." He brought his hand to the side of her face, and Caroline closed her eyes, delighting in the feel of his callused palm against her cheek. Smiling to herself at how far they'd come, she leaned into his hand.

"Do you think it'd wake Maggie if I kissed you?" he asked, whispering.

Caroline didn't know, but she was prepared to risk it. "I'm game if you are."

Still Grady hesitated. "This is the first time Maggie's been willing to have anything to do with me. I don't want to ruin that."

"If you don't kiss me *now*, Grady, I swear I'll never forgive you!"

He laughed softly and without further delay took her face between his hands. Once again Caroline shut her eyes, just for a moment, treasuring these rare moments of intimacy.

Slowly Grady bent toward her and she angled her head to accommodate his movement. His mouth was so close to hers. So close she could feel his breath against her skin. So close she could sense his longing—and admit her own. Yet he hesitated, as did she.

Caroline realized—and she suspected that Grady did, too—that everything between them would be forever changed if they proceeded with this kiss. It was more than an ordinary kiss. It was a meeting of two hearts, an admission of vulnerability and openness.

Caroline wasn't sure who moved first, but chose to think of what followed as a mutual decision. An inexorable drawing together.

The kiss was gentle, almost tentative. His hand drifted to the back of her neck, urging her forward.

Grady kissed her again, and this time his mouth was more demanding, more insistent. Within only a few seconds, Caroline felt as though she'd experienced every possible emotion. When he released her, his breath was ragged.

"I'm sorry, I—"

Rather than let him ruin everything with an apology, she kissed the corner of his mouth.

Maggie stirred and they both froze. Caroline prayed her daughter wouldn't awake, wouldn't unconsciously end these precious moments with Grady.

"Is she asleep?" he asked, speaking so quietly she had to strain to hear. His voice was more breath than sound.

"Yes…"

They waited breathlessly. When it seemed he wasn't going to kiss her again, Caroline took the initiative and leaned toward him. The strength of their attraction stunned her. It was as though they couldn't get close enough. Their mouths twisted and strained in a passionate desperate kiss, but that lasted only a moment.

Then sanity returned. Reluctantly they eased away from each other. Grady rested his shoulders against the seat cushion, tilted back his head and sighed deeply.

Caroline swallowed. "I'd better get Maggie inside," she whispered.

"Right." When he opened his door, the light blinded Caroline and she was grateful when he immediately closed it, making the least noise possible.

Coming around to her side, he opened the door, helped her out and then reached for Maggie, carrying her toward the house. Caroline had expected to carry Maggie herself. She'd always done so; she was accustomed to it. Grady's action brought to life a complexity of feelings—gratitude, relief, even a slight sense of loss.

"You get the door," Grady said.

Caroline unlocked the door. With only a night-light to guide them, she led him to Maggie's bedroom at the rear of the house. She folded back the covers on the bed and Grady carefully set the little girl down. Caroline removed her daughter's shoes and put them aside.

Grady smoothed the hair from Maggie's brow, touched his fingertips to his lips and pressed his hand to the little girl's brow. The gesture was so loving, so *fatherly,* that Caroline had to turn away.

Grady followed her into the darkened hallway. She continued to the front door. She didn't want him to leave but dared not ask him to stay.

"Thank you again," she whispered. "For everything." The front door remained open and light spilled in from the porch.

Grady didn't move.

Slowly she raised her eyes to his. The invitation was there, and it was simply beyond her to refuse him. He held his arms open. Less than four steps separated them, but she literally ran into his embrace. He caught her about the waist, and she wrapped her arms around his neck. They kissed again with an urgency that left her weak, an urgency that drained her of all thoughts save one—the unexpected wonder and joy she'd discovered in his arms.

Until that night, Caroline hadn't realized how lonely she'd been, how long the nights could be. In Grady's arms she felt whole and needed and beautiful.

When the kiss ended, she buried her face in his neck.

"I could hold you forever," he whispered.

"I could let you." She felt his smile.

"Don't tempt me more than I already am," he warned.

It was heaven knowing he found her attractive. He held her close while she struggled to regain her composure. Caroline was grateful for those few quiet moments before he slowly released her.

He placed his hands lightly on her shoulders. "I want to see you again."

"Yes." It didn't matter when or where.

"Soon."

She was almost giddy with the wonder of what was happening. "Please."

He smiled, and as though he couldn't help himself, he kissed her again.

Their kissing only seemed to get better and better. "Why did it take you so long?" she asked when she'd recovered enough to speak.

"Because I'm a pigheaded fool."

"I am, too." No need denying it. She was as much at fault as Grady.

"No more."

"No more," she echoed.

"Tomorrow," he suggested. "I can't wait any longer than that to see you again."

"Okay. When? Where?"

"Can you come out to the ranch?"

"Yes, of course. I'll come after church."

"Wonderful," he whispered, and kissed the tip of her nose. "Perfect."

She slipped her arms around his middle. "Oh, Grady, is this really happening or am I dreaming?"

"Nothing gets more real than the way you make me feel."

She smiled. Never would she have believed that Grady Weston was a romantic.

"About Maggie..."

He stiffened, and she stopped him by pressing her index finger against his lips. "Don't worry about her. Everything will work out."

"I don't mean to frighten her."

"I know."

"Did she like the flowers?"

Caroline kissed the underside of his jaw. "Very much."

"Did you?"

"More than I can say." She trailed kisses toward his ear and reveled in the way his body shuddered against hers when she tugged on his earlobe with her teeth.

"Caroline," he breathed. "You're making this impossible."

"Do I really tempt you?"

"Yes." His voice was low but harsh. "You don't have a clue."

Actually she did. "Kiss me one more time and then you can leave."

He hesitated, then gently captured her face between his hands and angled his mouth toward hers. The kiss, while one of need, was also one of elation, of shared joy. All this time they'd wasted, all the time they'd let pride and fear and doubt stand between them.

Caroline needed him and he needed her. Savannah, a woman with real insight into people, had tried to tell her that. And Caroline knew she'd tried to convince Grady, too. She was aware of Savannah's matchmaking efforts because her friend had told her; she was also aware that Savannah had been frustrated by one setback after another.

Caroline supposed she was as responsible for those setbacks as Grady. She'd always been attracted to him, but felt confused, unprepared. She'd been hurt terribly once and with that pain had come fear. For years she'd been afraid to love again. To trust again.

Deep within her, she recognized that Grady would never abandon her. Not Grady. He was as solid as a rock.

His final kiss was deep and long.

It took a moment for Maggie's voice to break through the fog of her desire.

"Mommy! Mommy!"

Grady groaned and reluctantly let Caroline go.

She turned to find Maggie standing in the dim light, rubbing the sleep from her eyes. "What is it, sweetheart?"

Maggie ignored the question and, instead, glared at Grady. "What are you doing to my mommy?" she demanded.

Chapter Four

Sunday morning was the one day of the week Jane Dickinson—*Dr.* Jane Dickinson, she reminded herself—could sleep in. Yet it was barely six and she was wide awake. Tossing aside the sheet, she threw on her robe and wandered barefoot into the kitchen.

"Texas," she muttered. Who would've believed when she signed up for this that she'd end up in the great state of Texas? The Hill Country was about as far as anyone could get from the bustling activity of Los Angeles.

Jane had *tried* to make a go of life in small-town America, but she was completely and utterly miserable. In three months she hadn't managed to make a single friend. Sure, there were lots of acquaintances, but no real friends. Never in her life had she missed her friends and family more, and all because of money. She'd entered into this agreement with the federal government in order to reduce her debts—three years in Promise, Texas, and her medical-school loans would be paid off.

Maybe she should just admit she'd made a mistake, pack her bags and hightail it out of this godforsaken town. But even as the thought entered her mind, Jane realized that wasn't what she wanted. What she wanted was to find some way to connect with these people, to become part of this tight-knit community.

The residents of Promise seemed willing enough to acknowledge that she was a competent physician specializing in family practice. But they came to see her only when they absolutely had to—for prescription renewals, a bad cough or sprain that couldn't be treated at home. Jane's one major fault was that she wasn't Dr. Cummings. The man had retired in his seventies after serving the community for nearly fifty years. The people of Promise knew and trusted him. She, on the other hand, was considered an outsider, and worse, some kind of Valley Girl or frivolous surfer type.

Despite her up-to-the-moment expertise, she had yet to gain the community's confidence. Everything she'd done to prove herself to the people of Promise had been a miserable failure.

Rejection wasn't something Jane was accustomed to dealing with. It left her feeling frustrated and helpless. In medical school, whenever she felt overwhelmed and emotionally confused, she'd gone jogging. It had always helped clear her thoughts, helped her gain perspective. But she hadn't hit the streets even once since she'd come here. With a new sense of resolve, she began to search for her running shoes, reminding herself that *she* was the one who'd agreed to work in a small community. She was determined to stick it out, even if it killed her.

Dressed in bright yellow nylon running shorts and a matching tank top, she started out at an easy nine-minute-mile pace. She jogged from her living quarters next to the health clinic down the tree-lined streets of Promise. The community itself wasn't so bad. Actually it was a pretty little town with traditional values and interesting people. Ranchers mostly. Down-to-earth folk, hardworking, family-oriented. That was what made her situation so difficult to understand. The people were friendly and welcoming, it seemed, to everyone but her.

Jane turned the corner onto Maple Street. At the post

office she took another turn and headed up Main. A couple of cars were parked in front of the bowling alley, which kept the longest hours in town; it was open twenty-four hours on Saturdays and Sundays. It wasn't the bowling that lured folks at all hours, but the café, which served good solid meals and great coffee at 1970s prices.

Jane's feet pounded the pavement and sweat rolled down the sides of her face. She'd barely gone a mile and already her body was suggesting that she hadn't been exercising enough. She knew she'd ache later but didn't care; she was already feeling more optimistic.

She rounded the corner off Main and onto Baxter, running past the antique store owned and operated by Dovie Boyd. Dovie lived in a brick home just around the corner. Despite the early hour, she was standing in the middle of her huge vegetable garden with her watering can in hand.

Jane had often admired the older woman's lush garden. The pole beans were six feet high, the tomatoes bursting with ripeness and the zucchini abundant. Jane marveled at how one woman could possible coax this much produce from a few plants.

"Morning," Jane called.

Dovie smiled and raised her hand in response.

Jane continued down the street, full steam ahead. She'd gone perhaps twenty yards when she realized it'd happened to her again. She'd never been a quitter in her life and she wasn't going to start now. She did an abrupt about-face and headed back.

Dovie looked surprised to see her.

Jane stopped and, breathing heavily, leaned forward and braced her hands on her knees. "Hello again," she said when she'd caught her breath.

Without a pause Dovie continued watering. "Lovely morning, isn't it?"

"Beautiful," Jane agreed. Slowly she straightened and

watched Dovie expertly weave her way through the garden, pausing now and again to finger a plant or pull a weed.

"Do you have a minute, Mrs. Boyd?" she asked, gathering her nerve. She rested her hands against the white picket fence.

Widening her eyes, Dovie turned. "What can I do for you, Dr. Dickinson?"

"First, I'd like it if you called me Jane."

"Then Jane it is."

The older woman's tone was friendly, but Jane sensed the same reserve in her she'd felt in others.

"What am I doing wrong?" She hadn't intended to blurt out the question like that, but couldn't help herself.

"Wrong?" Dovie set the watering can aside.

"What's wrong with *me?*" she amended.

"I don't think anything's wrong with you." The other woman was clearly puzzled by the question. "What makes you assume such a thing?"

Attitudes were so difficult to describe. How could she explain how she felt without sounding snobbish or self-pitying? But she had to try.

"Why am I standing on this side of the fence while you're on that side?" Jane asked as she paced the cement walkway. "Why do I have to be the one to greet others first? People don't like me, and I want to know why."

Dovie lifted one finger to her lips and frowned, apparently deep in thought. "You did greet me first, didn't you?"

"Yes, but it isn't only you. It's everyone." Jane paused, struggling with her composure. "I want to know why."

"My goodness, I'm not sure. I never realized." Dovie walked toward the short white gate and unlatched it, swinging it open. "Come inside, dear, and we'll sit down and reason this out."

Now that Jane had made her point, it would have been

rude and unfair to refuse, but to her embarrassment she discovered she was close to tears.

"Sit down and make yourself comfortable," Dovie said, and gestured toward the white wrought-iron patio set. "I'll get a pot of tea brewing. I don't know about you, but I tend to think more clearly if I have something hot to drink."

"I… Thank you," Jane said, feeling humble and grateful at once. The few moments Dovie was in the kitchen gave her time to collect herself.

Soon Dovie reappeared carrying a tray with a pot of steaming tea and two delicate china cups, as well as a plate of scones. She set it down on the table and poured the tea, handing Jane the first cup.

Jane felt a bit conspicuous in her tank top, sipping tea from a Spode cup, but she was too thankful for Dovie's kindness to worry about it.

"All right now," Dovie said when she'd finished pouring. "Let's talk." she sat down and leaned back in her chair, pursing her lips. "Tell me some other things that have bothered you about Promise."

Jane wasn't sure where to start. "I have this…this sense that people don't like me."

"Nonsense," Dovie countered. "We don't know you well enough to like or dislike you."

"You're right. No one knows me," Jane murmured. "I need a friend," she said with a shrug, offering the one solution that had come to her.

"We all need friends, but perhaps you need to make more of an effort to give people a chance to know you."

"But I *have* tried to meet people," she said in her own defense.

Dovie frowned. "Give me an example."

Jane had a list of those. An inventory of failures cataloged from the day she'd first arrived. "The party for Richard Weston,'' she said. It was the first social event she'd attended in the area. Richard had been warm and friendly, stopping her on the street and issuing a personal invitation. Jane had been excited about it, had even told her family she was attending the party. But when she got there, she'd ended up standing around by herself. The evening had been uncomfortable from the start.

As the new doctor in town Jane appeared to be a topic of speculation and curiosity. The short newspaper article published about her earlier in the week had added to the attention she'd garnered. People stared at her, a few had greeted her, asked her a question or two, then drifted away. Richard had been the star of his own party, and the one time he'd noticed her, she was sure he'd forgotten who she was. For a while she'd wandered around, feeling awkward and out of place. Mostly she'd felt like a party crasher and left soon after she'd arrived.

''You *were* there, weren't you?'' Dovie murmured with a thoughtful look.

''Yes.'' Not that it'd done Jane any good.

''You came in a suit and high heels, as I recall,'' Dovie added.

''I realized as soon as I arrived the suit was a mistake,'' Jane said. At the time she'd felt it was important to maintain a professional image. She was new in town and attempting to make a good impression.

''And then jeans and a cotton top to the Grange dance.''

''I didn't realize it was a more formal affair.'' She hadn't lasted long there, either. ''I wasn't sure what to wear,'' Jane confessed. She'd come overdressed for one event and underdressed for the other. ''But,'' she said hopelessly, ''I had no way of knowing.''

Dovie nodded, silently encouraging her to continue.

''I showed up for the Willie Nelson Fourth of July picnic, too, but no one bothered to tell me Willie Nelson wouldn't be there." That had been a major disappointment, as well.

Dovie giggled and shook her head. "The town council's invited him nine years running, and he's politely declined every year, but we've never let a little thing like that stand in our way. This is Willie Nelson country!"

"Someone might have said something." Jane didn't take kindly to being the only one not in on the joke.

"That's something you can only learn by living here. Next year, you'll know."

If I'm here that long, Jane thought.

"Another thing," she said. "What's all this about a ghost town?" Jane asked next.

Dovie's expressive eyes narrowed. "Who told you there was a ghost town?"

Jane wondered at the swift change in her newfound friend. "I overheard two children talking. One of them mentioned it."

"Don't pay any attention to those rumors, understand?"

"Is there one?"

"That's neither here nor there," Dovie said, but not unkindly. "We have other more important matters to discuss."

"Such as?"

Dovie's head came back. "You." Her face was set, her voice firm. "You're right, you do need a friend."

"Are you volunteering to take me under your wing?" Jane asked, and hoped Dovie understood how very grateful she'd be.

"I'm too old." Dovie's response was fast. "I'm thinking of someone more your age." She tapped her index finger against her chin. "You and Ellie Frasier would get along like gangbusters. Unfortunately Ellie's busy getting ready for her wedding just now, so you'll need to be patient."

"Oh." Jane's voice was small.

"Until then, you and I have our work cut out for us."

Jane frowned, not sure she understood. "What work?"

Dovie's expression told Jane she'd overlooked the obvious. "We need to find out what's wrong with everyone in this town. I've decided there's nothing wrong with *you*, Dr. Jane. It's everyone else, and I'm determined to find out what."

"ALL THE COMFORTS of home," Richard Weston said out loud. He stood in the middle of the dirt road that ran through the ghost town. "Bitter End, Texas," he continued, "population one." He laughed then, the sound echoing down the long dusty street littered with sagebrush and rock.

Hitching his thumbs in the waistband of his jeans, he sauntered down the dirt road as if he owned it, and for all intents and purposes, he did.

For the time being Bitter End was his home. He was proud of the good job he'd done carving out a comfortable place for himself. He figured he'd be stuck here for a while. How long wasn't clear yet. A man on the run didn't have a lot of alternatives.

Everything was about to catch up with him. His brother already knew he hadn't paid that old coot Max Jordan, and he wasn't going to be able to hide all the other charges he'd made, either. Although Grady's business account had sure come in handy. But he'd stretched his luck to the max in Promise.

Time to move on. Hide again, only no one would ever think to look for him here. He was as safe as a babe cuddled in his mother's loving arms. Richard had a sixth sense about when to walk away. He'd come to trust his instincts; they were what had kept him out of prison this long.

Richard kicked the toe of his snakeskin boot into the hard dry ground. He'd arrived in Promise penniless, miserable and afraid to glance over his shoulder for fear the law—or worse—was hot on his tail. He'd decided to head back to Promise on the spur of the moment, when he awoke one morning and found himself outside El Paso without money or transportation. Hitchhiking, he made his way to the central part of the state.

Luck had blessed him all his life. He hadn't been back long before he discovered Savannah had visited Bitter End. As soon as his older sister mentioned the ghost town, he'd known what to do.

Little by little Richard had managed to squirrel away supplies, making the trek so often he no longer lost his way. Each day he managed to take something from the ranch or buy supplies on ranch credit. In the beginning it was little things, items not easily missed. Seldom-used equipment no one would notice was gone. Gradually he'd worked in the larger pricier necessities. He'd been clever about it, too.

Still congratulating himself, Richard walked up the old wooden steps to the boardwalk. He sat down in the rocking chair he'd discovered in one of the buildings and surveyed the town. His domain.

He'd been born under a lucky star, Richard told himself, and its shine hadn't faded. He marveled anew at the crafty way he'd charged much of what he needed. Grady didn't have a clue, either. Richard would charge something nonsensical like tractor parts to Grady's account, knowing no one would think to question that. Later, making sure it wasn't the same salesclerk, he'd return the part and use the credit to purchase what he really needed. In the weeks since his return he'd accumulated all the comforts of home, and the best part was that it had been at his brother's expense.

"Oh, yes, I'm going to be real comfortable now," he said, grinning broadly. Tucking his hands behind his head, he leaned back. "Thanks, Grady," he said with a snicker.

Slowly his smile faded. None of this hiding out would be necessary if the situation with Ellie Frasier had worked out differently. It would have been easy to let that sweet young thing soothe away his worries, but his hopes had died a humiliating death, thanks to Glen Patterson.

Why any woman would choose some cowboy over him was beyond Richard. Clearly Ellie had no taste. In the beginning he'd been drawn to the inheritance her daddy had left her, figuring he'd talk her into marrying him, get his hands on the money and then skip town.

As time progressed and he came to know Ellie, he'd actually found himself thinking about sticking around and making a go of life in Promise. Money in the right places would put an end to his current troubles. For a while he'd toyed with the idea of getting involved in local politics. Promise could use a mayor like him, not some hick but a man with an eye to the future. Then maybe for once he'd be able to stay out of trouble, make a new life for himself. Start over. But unfortunately it hadn't panned out.

Standing, Richard glanced at his watch. He hadn't moved here yet, so he had to be conscious of the time. Although his sister and brother hadn't said much, they were aware of his absences, and he didn't want to arouse their suspicions.

Richard headed to where he'd parked the pickup. After several failed attempts, he'd found a new way into the town, one that didn't necessitate a long walk.

The wind whistled behind him, a low plaintive cry that sent shivers down his spine.

''Oh, no, you don't,'' he said. Naturally there'd been talk about ghosts in Bitter End. The one time he'd brought Ellie with him, she'd been squirming out of her skin in her eagerness to leave. She claimed it was a feeling she had, a sense of oppression. His sister had said she, too, could feel something weird in the old town.

Yeah, right.

Not Richard, at least not until that very moment. The

wind increased in velocity, whistling as he walked away, his back to the main street.

"I don't hear anything, I don't feel anything," he said aloud, more in an effort to hear the words than to convince himself.

The sensation, or whatever the hell it was, didn't dissipate until he was safe inside his brother's dilapidated truck. With the doors locked Richard relaxed, suspecting he'd viewed one too many episodes of "Tales from the Crypt."

As he drove off, another thought entered his mind.

Caroline Daniels.

He had no real interest in her himself, but he could have her and he knew it. His brother was sweet on Caroline; that was easy to guess, just from the way Grady looked at her. It might be rotten of him, Richard thought with a grin, but he sure did love to play the spoilsport.

His brother had as much charisma as an overripe tomato, yet Grady was the one sitting pretty on a prosperous ranch, living high, while Richard had to worry about where his next meal was coming from. Some things in life just weren't fair, and if he wanted to even them out a little, he could see no harm in it. Besides, he subscribed to the idea that, regardless of the star he was born under, a man made his own luck. Or, at least, enhanced it.

"You don't know how good you've got it, big brother," Richard said. It shouldn't be hard to lure Caroline away from Grady—and it didn't hurt any that her kid was crazy about him. Kids had always liked him, and Richard had encouraged them. For some reason a lot of people put stock in their kids' opinions and preferences. As far as he was concerned, it didn't matter a damn what some kid thought, although he didn't mind using a child to manipulate the parent.

Maggie was a great example. She preferred him over Grady, which made him the leading man when it came to winning her mother's affections. He found Caroline kind of irritating, though; he didn't care for the way she looked at him.

What he enjoyed most of all was playing himself off against his brother. He loved it when he could frustrate Grady, but his older brother made it much too easy; he took all the fun out of it. Well, not *all* the fun. Poor old Grady—would he never learn? Richard smirked. When he was around, Grady didn't stand a chance with the ladies.

GRADY FELT LIKE A KID waiting for prom night—a kid who had a date with the prom queen. The chance to see Caroline again was worth cutting short his sleep. It meant getting up earlier than usual to deal with morning chores. But he'd managed, surprising Wade as much as he did Savannah and Laredo when he slipped into the pew two minutes before services were due to start.

He hadn't come to hear the sermon, but he figured God would forgive that. He'd come for Caroline. She sang with the choir, and the possibility of seeing her again so soon after the church dinner was irresistible.

Grady still walked on air after last night's kisses. Even Maggie's interruption hadn't ruined the evening. He'd been at a loss for words when she'd stumbled upon Caroline and him with their arms locked around each other. Rather than try to explain, he'd left the matter in Caroline's capable hands and departed soon afterward.

The last thing she'd said before he walked out the door was that she'd stop by the ranch Sunday afternoon.

Mere hours away.

The service was upbeat, and Wade's message caused him to nod his head in agreement a number of times. The minister used humor and lots of anecdotes, which made for an interesting sermon. Before he realized it, the hour was over and the congregation dismissed with a benediction.

Pastor Wade McMillen stood in the doorway as people left. "Good to see you, Grady," he said, giving Grady's hand a hearty shake. "But somehow I don't think it was my sermon that interested you."

Grady grumbled some noncommittal reply. Damned little escaped Wade's attention. As if to prove him right, Wade caught Jeremy Bishop by the shoulder, stopping him on his way out the door.

"That must have been an interesting book you were reading in church," he said with an encouraging smile.

Jeremy squirmed uncomfortably before he reached inside his shirt. With obvious reluctance he withdrew a slim paperback novel.

"T. R. Grant?" Wade said, and cocked one eyebrow at the title.

Jeremy's eyes grew round. "You've never heard of T. R. Grant?"

"Can't say I have," Wade admitted.

"He's great!"

Wade chuckled. "I'm sure he is. Maybe I should read him, too."

"I've read everything he's ever written. I can lend you one of his books if you want."

"I'll take you up on that offer." Wade ruffled the boy's hair and returned his attention to Grady. "I see that things are developing nicely between you and Caroline Daniels."

Grady tensed. He had no desire to discuss his private life.

As if he knew that, too, Wade slapped him lightly on the back. "It took you long enough," he said with a laugh. Before Grady could respond, Wade had begun talking to someone else.

Grady met Caroline on the front lawn. He saw her speak to Wade, then glance at him, smiling shyly. The yard was crowded with people visiting and chatting, but everyone appeared to fade from sight as Caroline approached.

"Hello again," he said, which was probably the stupidest thing he'd ever uttered. Not that he cared.

"Hello." Her voice had a deep breathless quality.

"Were you able to reassure Maggie?" He'd felt bad about leaving her to make the explanations, but feared any effort on his part wouldn't have come out right.

"She understands."

"But does she approve?"

Caroline's eyes avoided his, which was answer enough in itself. "It isn't up to Maggie to approve or disapprove of whom I kiss."

He exhaled slowly and would have said more except that he couldn't stop looking at Caroline. She was so damn pretty, any coherent thought didn't stand a chance of lasting more than a second or two. It was her eyes, he concluded, a deep rich shade of chocolate. No, he decided after a moment, it was her soft brown hair. He remembered the silky feel of it bunched in his hands when he'd kissed her. He remembered a whole lot more than the feel of her hair....

"So you're coming to see Savannah this afternoon?" he asked, trying to redirect his thoughts. If he continued in this vein much longer, he'd end up kissing her right then and there just to prove how real last night had been.

"No."

Grady's disappointment was sharp. "You're not? But I thought—"

"I'm coming to see you."

His heart, which had gone sluggish with discouragement, sped up, and he could feel his pulse hammering in his neck.

"Hi, Grady," Maggie said, joining her mother. She clung to her mother's arm and looked up at him with a slight frown.

"Hi, Maggie. I hear you're coming out to the ranch this afternoon."

The child continued to stare at him, and although she made no comment, Grady saw the way she moved protectively close to her mother.

"Did Savannah tell you about the new colt we have?"

She nodded.

"He's only a few days old, but he's already handsome. I bet you'd like to see him."

Again she nodded.

Grady glanced at Caroline. "Do you think Maggie's old enough to visit the colt?"

"I can, can't I, Mommy?" Maggie twisted around and gazed up at her mother with imploring eyes.

"I think it should be all right, as long as you stay with Grady."

"I will, I will," she promised.

"That new colt needs a name," Grady added. "Maybe you could help us decide what to call him."

Her eyes got huge. "Could I really?"

"If you can think of a decent name for such a handsome boy. We'll let you take a gander at him first, pet him a few times and then give you the opportunity to think up a name."

"That's kind of you, Grady," Caroline said.

They walked toward the parking lot, in no particular hurry. "What time will you be by, do you think?" he asked, restraining himself from suggesting she should come right that minute.

"Maggie needs lunch and a nap first."

"She can eat with us—you both could—and then Maggie could nap. Savannah'll be more than happy to watch her." After she finished wringing his neck for inviting company without consulting her first. "While Maggie's resting, perhaps you and I could..." For the life of him, he couldn't think of a single respectable thing for the two of them to do.

"Go riding," Caroline inserted. "I'll borrow some jeans from Savannah."

She could have suggested mud wrestling and he would've agreed.

"Well…I suppose we can alter our plans just a little," Caroline said, smiling softly.

It took a moment for the words to sink into his consciousness. "You could? Great."

"Are we going to Savannah's?" Maggie asked, tugging at the sleeve of her mother's dress. "Are we leaving now?"

"It looks that way," Caroline answered.

Maggie clapped her hands, celebrating the good news.

"I'll see you there, then," she said to Grady, opening the passenger door for Maggie. Her daughter leaped inside, eager to be on their way.

Grady opened the driver's side for Maggie. "Drive carefully."

She got in and assured him she would.

Grady stepped away from the car when she started the engine; he watched her back out of the parking space and turn out of the driveway before he realized that he'd attracted a number of curious stares. In particular, he noticed Edwina and Lily Moorhouse studying him.

The two sisters were retired teachers, as prim and proper as the spinster schoolmarms of nineteenth-century Promise. They smiled approvingly in his direction before they leaned toward one another, heads close enough to touch, talking up a storm. He'd been in their classes as a boy and could well recall the speed with which those two could chatter. Two hundred words a minute, he guessed, with gusts up to four fifty.

Their tongues were wagging now, but frankly, Grady didn't care. He was about to spend the afternoon with the woman who'd dominated his thoughts for months. The woman who dominated his dreams.

Grady arrived back at the Yellow Rose less than five minutes behind Caroline. He found her in the kitchen with Savannah, preparing Sunday dinner. She paused when he entered, then glanced around her.

"Did you see Maggie?"

"Maggie?" He shook his head.

"She wasn't on the porch?"

"Not that I noticed." He stuck his head out the door and couldn't see her.

"I told her not to leave the porch." Caroline sighed with impatience. She set aside the tomato she was slicing and reached for a towel.

"She came to me for a carrot not more than a minute ago," Savannah said.

"She probably went into the barn to see the new colt." Grady blamed himself for that.

"She knows better," Caroline murmured. "It's not safe there."

"Don't worry, she's only been gone a minute," Savannah said reassuringly.

"I'll get her," Grady offered, eager to prove to Maggie that he could be as charming and wonderful as Richard.

"Are you sure you don't mind?" Caroline asked.

"Not in the least." Grady headed toward the barn, whistling as he went. The interior was dark after the bright sunlight, and he squinted until his eyes adjusted to the change in lighting.

"Maggie," he called out.

No answer.

"Maggie," he called again.

A soft almost mewing sound followed. Grady whirled around. The noise came from Widowmaker's stall. When he looked inside, Grady's heart froze. Maggie was huddled against the wall, her face white with terror.

Just then, the ill-tempered stallion thrashed out with his hooves, narrowly missing the child.

Chapter Five

Grady knew that he had to make his move fast or Maggie could be seriously hurt. Widowmaker snorted and began to paw the floor. Unwilling to give the stallion an opportunity to get any closer to the child, Grady threw open the stall door, grabbed Maggie and literally swung her out of harm's way.

Maggie let out a scream. With his heart pounding, Grady firmly held the squirming child against him, trying to comfort her and at the same time calm his own fears. Unfortunately he failed on both counts.

The barn door flew open and Savannah and Caroline rushed breathlessly inside.

''Mommy! Mommy!''

Grady released Maggie, who raced toward her mother, nearly stumbling in her eagerness to escape his clutches. Caroline held her arms open and the child sobbed hysterically as she fell into her mother's embrace.

''What happened?'' Savannah asked.

''Somehow Maggie got into Widowmaker's stall,'' Grady explained. His knees shook so badly he sank onto a bale of hay.

''Dear God,'' Savannah whispered, and lowered herself onto the bale beside him. ''Is she hurt?''

Grady didn't think so.

Caroline's eyes were filled with questions, but it was impossible to talk over the sound of Maggie's crying.

"What about you?" Savannah asked. "You didn't get kicked, did you?"

"I'm fine." Which wasn't entirely true. Grady figured just seeing Maggie in that stall cost him five years of his life. God only knew what would have happened if he hadn't gotten there when he had. The thought wasn't one he wished to entertain.

Gathering the child in her arms, Caroline made her way out of the barn. Savannah and Grady followed. His sister returned to the house, but Grady lingered outside, not knowing how to help although he wanted to do *something*. He waited for a clue from Caroline, who sat on one of the porch steps as she cradled her daughter. Maggie continued to sob almost uncontrollably, hiding her face in her mother's shoulder. Caroline stopped whispering to the child and started to sing in a low soothing voice gently swaying back and forth.

Grady pulled out the rocking chair and Caroline's eyes revealed her gratitude as she sat down in it. When the song was finished, she talked softly to Maggie, reassuring the little girl once more that everything was fine and there was nothing to be afraid of.

Grady paced the area in front of the porch, waiting, wondering what he should do next. If anything. Gradually Maggie quieted. Then she straightened and glanced around.

"Hello, princess," he said, remembering that was what his father had called Savannah. It seemed to suit Maggie. "Are you okay?"

Maggie took one look at him and burst into tears. Within seconds she'd buried her face in her mother's shoulder again.

"What'd I say?" he asked, unable to understand what he'd done now. He'd hoped the child would view him as her hero since he'd saved her from certain harm. Apparently that wasn't the case.

"She's embarrassed," Caroline explained.

"Embarrassed?" he shouted, forgetting how his booming voice terrified the little girl. Maggie burrowed deeper into her mother's embrace.

Savannah opened the screen door and stepped onto the porch. "Dinner's ready if anyone's interested," she announced.

Grady wasn't. His appetite was gone. Conflicting emotions churned in him—he felt angry and relieved, frustrated and pleased, confused and happy. He wanted to hug Maggie and thank God she was safe, and at the same time chastise her for giving him the fright of his life.

"I think it might be best if I took Maggie home," Caroline said.

"No." Grady's protest was instantaneous. "I mean, you need to do what you think is best but…" He didn't know what he wanted other than to spend time with her, but now it seemed that wasn't going to happen.

"I'll see if I can settle her down," Caroline offered. She held Maggie in her arms and continued to rock, humming softly.

Grady sat on the top step and marveled at her gentle manner with the child. The way she calmed Maggie helped quiet his own heart. No one seemed to realize it, but he'd suffered quite a jolt himself. Rocket sat next to him, his head nestled on Grady's lap. The old dog had belonged to his father, and in the years since his parents' deaths, Grady had spent many a late-night sitting quietly with Rocket. Talking a bit, mostly just thinking. The dog had often comforted him.

When he was sure he wouldn't disturb the child's slumber, Grady dragged the vacant rocker next to Caroline.

"Thank you," she whispered. Reaching out, she

squeezed his hand. "I hate to think what could have happened if you hadn't arrived when you did. Maggie knows better. I'll have a talk with her later, but I don't think you need to worry about anything like this again. I don't believe I've ever seen her so frightened."

"I was terrified myself." He wasn't ashamed to admit it.

Caroline closed her eyes as though to shake the image of her daughter in the stallion's stall from her mind.

It was difficult for Grady not to stare at her.

"Go and have your dinner," she said a moment later. "I'm only going to stay a few more minutes."

"I'm not hungry," he said, wishing he could convince her to stay.

"I'm sorry, Grady, for everything."

He gestured with one hand, dismissing her apology.

"I was looking forward to riding with you this afternoon," she said.

He'd forgotten the ostensible reason for her visit. He shrugged as if it was no big thing. "We'll do it some other time."

She brushed the hair away from Maggie's sweet face. "I'd better go."

The screen door opened and Savannah poked her head out. "Do you want to put Maggie down on my bed?" she asked. "I'll watch her so you two can…" She didn't finish the statement, but Grady knew his sister. She'd been about to say, "so you two can have some time alone together."

Caroline shook her head. "Maggie's had a terrible fright and she's embarrassed because she knows she did wrong. I need to talk to her and it'd be best if I did that at home."

"I'll walk you to your car," Grady offered. He stuffed his hands in his back pockets as he stood up.

"I'm so sorry, Savannah," Caroline whispered.

"I'll see you again soon, won't I?"

"Of course."

Savannah and Grady walked down the porch steps with Caroline holding the sleeping Maggie. "Laredo and I are driving into Fredericksburg to talk to our builder next Wednesday. If everything goes according to plan, we'll be in our own home by October."

The house would be empty without Savannah, but Grady refused to think about it. At least her new home wouldn't be far from the ranch house, no more than a five-minute walk.

"The house plans are ready?"

Savannah looked inordinately proud. "Laredo and I finished going over everything Friday afternoon and gave our approval to the builder. You can't imagine how much time and effort went into that."

They reached the car, and Grady opened the passenger door so Caroline could set Maggie down. The child didn't so much as stir when Caroline placed the seat belt around her.

"Seeing as Laredo and I will be gone most of Wednesday, perhaps that would be a good day for you two to get together." Savannah made the suggestion casually, as though she often arranged her brother's schedule.

"Ah…" Grady was a little embarrassed by her obviousness.

"I can come over after work," Caroline said, smiling at him. "But I don't know if the sitter can keep Maggie."

"Bring her with you," Savannah said. "That'll give the three of you time together. It's important for Maggie to feel comfortable around Grady."

He was warming to the idea. "Perhaps we could all go riding," he said. "I've got a nice, gentle horse I'll put you and Maggie on." He thought it would be fun to show them the herd and stop at a few special spots along the way. He was proud of the Yellow Rose.

"That would be wonderful!" Caroline sounded enthusiastic; her voice and movements seemed animated, even excited.

"Then it's a date," Grady said.

"I'll see you soon." Savannah turned to leave, hurrying back to the house.

Grady and Caroline stood in the yard, and Maggie slept on contentedly as a cool breeze passed through the open door.

"I'd better get going," Caroline said.

Grady noticed the reluctance in her words, felt it himself. "I'm glad we had a little time together, anyway."

"Me, too."

There was a moment's silence, then Caroline did something completely out of character, something that stunned him. Without warning, she stepped forward and kissed him.

Caught by surprise, Grady was slow to react. A second later he clasped her in his arms, so deeply involved in the kiss that he didn't care *who* saw them. Even Richard.

Neither one of them was able to breathe properly when the kiss ended. Their balance seemed to be affected, too. Grady gripped her elbows and she held on to his waist.

Their eyes met and she smiled the softest, sweetest, sexiest smile he'd ever seen.

"What was that for?" he asked, his voice thick with passion.

"For saving Maggie."

"Oh." He cleared his throat. "I once saved a wounded falcon."

She kissed his cheek.

"It was hurt real bad."

Her lips inched closer to his.

"Richard broke his arm when he was eight and I carried him home. Will you reward me with a kiss for that, as well?"

"Grady!" she protested with a laugh. "Enough."

He loved the sound of her laughter. Because he wanted to hold her one last time, he scooped her into his arms and swung her around. Throwing back her head, she continued to laugh with such sheer joy it infected his very soul. They hugged for a long time afterward, content simply to be in each other's arms.

This was heaven, Grady told himself. Heaven in its purest form.

GLEN WAS AT FRASIER FEED early Tuesday evening just as he'd promised. Ellie'd had a long grueling day; not only was the store exceptionally busy, their wedding was less than a month away and there was an endless list of things that needed to be done.

"I'm glad you're on time," she said, smiling at him, loving him. She marveled again at how they'd both been so incredibly blind to their feelings. Obtuse was the word for the pair of them.

"Hey, when was I ever late?" Glen teased.

Ellie rolled her eyes and hung the Closed sign in the shop window. She started toward the office where she kept her purse, but hadn't gone far when Glen caught her hand and stopped her.

"Not so soon. Aren't you going to let me know how pleased you are to see me?"

"I see you every day," she reminded him.

"We aren't even married and already you're treating me like an old hat." He wore a woebegone look.

Laughing, Ellie locked her arms around his neck and gave him a kiss he wouldn't soon forget. Neither would she.

"Oh, baby," he whispered, his eyes closed. "How much longer until the wedding?"

"Less than a month." Her head buzzed with everything

they still needed to do, to decide and plan. "Sometimes I wish we could just run away and get married."

"That idea appeals to me more and more," he murmured.

Ellie was tempted herself, but reason soon took over. "Your mother and mine would never forgive us."

"In that case, let's live in sin and give them something to really be upset about."

Despite herself, Ellie giggled. "You always make me laugh."

"I'm glad to know you find me a source of entertainment."

"Always," she joked, kissing him again, lightly this time.

He released her with a reluctance that warmed her heart. Ellie retrieved her purse from the office and tucked in her to-do list.

"When are we scheduled to meet with the Realtor?" Glen asked.

"Not until seven." Where they would live had been a major decision. If she moved out to the ranch with Glen and Cal, she'd be commuting to Promise each day. If Glen moved into town, then he'd be the one commuting. In the end they'd decided to buy a house in town. Glen would continue working with his brother for a number of years, but hoped someday to start his own spread. When the time came, they'd buy a ranch closer to town, but that was years in the future.

Glen checked his watch. "Do we have time for a quick bite to eat?"

"If you want."

He growled. "I'm starving."

"All right, cowboy, let's stop at the Chili Pepper for a quick sandwich."

Only a few months ago Ellie's life had been empty

enough to swallow her whole. Her father had died, and then her mother had unexpectedly sold the family home and moved to Chicago. For the first time in her life Ellie had been utterly alone. That was when she realized how much she'd come to rely on her best friend—and eventually know how much she loved him.

They walked to the restaurant and managed to get a booth. Both were familiar enough with the menu not to need one. Ellie ordered the barbecue sandwich and a side of potato salad, and Glen chose a slab of the baby back ribs. He also asked for a pitcher of ice-cold beer.

"Dovie took me to lunch this afternoon," Ellie said when the beer arrived.

"Anything going on with her these days?"

"She wanted to know how the wedding plans were coming along, and…" Ellie hesitated.

"And?" he prodded, pouring them each a beer.

"Have you met Dr. Dickinson yet?"

"Doc Cumming's replacement? Not officially. Why?"

"Dovie asked if I'd, you know, take her under my wing."

"The doctor?" Glen set his mug down on the table.

"Apparently she's not adjusting to life in Promise."

Glen relaxed against the red vinyl upholstery. "How do you mean?"

"She doesn't fit in, and Dovie seems to think what she really needs is a friend, someone to introduce her to people, show her the ropes."

"Do you have time for this?" Glen asked, zeroing in on Ellie's own concern.

"Not just now."

"Don't think you're going to have a lot of spare time once we're married, either," he said with a twinkle in his eyes. "I plan on keeping you occupied myself."

"Oh, really?" Although she enjoyed bantering with him, Ellie could feel the heat rise in her cheeks.

"What that doctor really needs is something or someone to occupy her time."

"I suppose you're going to suggest a man," Ellie said.

"You got something against men?"

"Just a minute." Ellie put down her mug too quickly, then used her napkin to wipe up the spilled beer. "You just might be on to something here."

Glen frowned. "What do you mean?"

"Why don't we introduce the new doc to Cal?" An idea was beginning to take shape in her mind, and fast gaining momentum.

"My brother?" Glen sounded incredulous.

"Yes, your brother!" She snorted. "Do you know any other Cal?"

Glen stared at her as if seeing her for the first time. "You're not serious, are you?"

"Yes, I am. They're perfect for each other."

Glen slapped the side of his head, pretending there was something wrong with his hearing. "Let me get this straight. The woman I love, the very one who couldn't see the forest for the trees, is about to take on the role of matchmaker."

"It only makes sense."

"You haven't even *met* the woman."

"I most certainly have," Ellie protested.

"When?"

"The Cattlemen's Association dance," she informed him primly, neglecting to mention that it had been a ten-second conversation and they'd done nothing more than exchange first names.

"Okay, Ms. Romance Expert, explain to me why you think my brother should meet this Mary."

"Her name is Jane."

"Jane," he corrected. "What's so special about her?"

"I don't know," Ellie was forced to admit. "But I do know one thing...."

"What's that?"

"Cal needs someone."

Their meal arrived and Glen reached for a blackened rib and dipped it in the pungent smoky barbecue sauce that was Adam Braunfels's speciality. "Does Cal know his life is lacking?" he asked.

"Not yet."

"Are you going to tell him, or are you volunteering me for the job?"

Glen appeared to find her idea highly entertaining, but she ignored his unwarranted amusement. "Neither of us will need to tell him," she said.

Glen made a show of wiping the sweat from his brow. "Boy, am I relieved."

"Cal will discover this all on his own."

"Listen, honey, I hate to burst your bubble, but Cal's a confirmed bachelor. I don't even remember the last time he went out on a date. He's sworn off women for good."

"You sure about that?"

"Well, it's been more than two years now, and he still isn't over Jennifer."

"Then it's about time he *got* over her." She sounded more confident than she felt, but she wasn't going to let a little thing like male pride stand in her way. Cal needed someone in his life, but he was too stubborn to realize it. Like most of the male sex he simply needed a little help. She'd aim him in the right direction and leave matters to progress as they would.

Eventually Cal *would* see the light; he'd figure it out on his own. As soon as she and Glen were married, Cal would be in that ranch house all by himself. It wouldn't take him long to discover how large and lonely a house could be with just one person living there.

"You look thoughtful," Glen said.

"It's going to be up to us." She nodded firmly.

"Us?" He raised both hands. "Not me! Forget it. If you want to play matchmaker with my big brother, you go right ahead, but don't include me."

A little respect for the validity of her idea—bringing two lonely people together—would have gone a long way, but Glen was having none of it.

"Good luck, sweetheart," he said, reaching for a French fry. "I have to admire your spirit.'

"I don't believe in luck," she told him with the confidence of one who knows. "I believe we shape our own destinies." *And occasionally someone else's.*

LATE WEDNESDAY AFTERNOON Caroline drove into the yard of the Yellow Rose Ranch. She'd been looking forward to this all week.

As she parked, the screen door opened off the back porch and Grady stepped outside.

Caroline climbed out of the car, and Maggie slipped her small hand into Caroline's as he approached.

"Will Grady yell at me?" Maggie whispered.

"Of course not," Caroline assured her.

Grady smiled at them and it was difficult for Caroline to look away. His face was alight with such pleasure she had to catch her breath. They'd known each other for years, she and Grady; they had a history, most of it unpleasant. Both were opinionated, strong willed. But she'd always admired Grady, always thought him honorable and decent. She'd carefully guarded her heart for a lot of years, and he was the first man, the only man, to get close enough to make her dream again.

"Hi," she said, feeling self-conscious.

"Hello." His gaze left her and traveled to Maggie. He bent down on one knee to be eye to eye with Caroline's daughter. "How are you, princess?"

"Fine." Maggie kicked at the dirt with the toe of her shoe and lowered her head to stare at the ground. "I'm sorry I went into the big horse's stall."

"You were looking for the colt, weren't you?"

Maggie nodded and kept her head lowered. When she spoke, even Caroline had trouble understanding her. "I won't do it again."

"Good for you," Grady said. "It's a wise woman who learns from her mistakes."

"And man," Caroline added.

Grady threw back his head and laughed loudly. At the sound Maggie leaped two feet off the ground and flew into her mother's arms, her own small arms tight around Caroline's neck.

"What'd you say to her this time?" Richard asked as he sauntered out of the bunkhouse.

"Richard!" Maggie twisted around, her face wreathed in smiles.

"How's my cupcake?" Richard asked, holding out his arms to the youngster.

Maggie squirmed free of Caroline's embrace and hurried toward the other man. Richard cheerfully caught her, lifted her high above his head and swung her around. Maggie shouted with glee.

"What are you doing here?" Grady asked, frowning.

The smile on Richard's face faded. "This is my home."

"Not anymore. Nothing here belongs to you."

The message was clear. Grady was telling his younger brother to keep away from Caroline and Maggie.

Richard laughed as if to say the mere suggestion was ludicrous. "How can you bar me from something that was never yours?'' he asked. He switched his attention to Maggie.

"Maggie, I think—'' Caroline started, but was interrupted.

"I like Richard!'' her daughter cried. "Not Grady, *Richard.*''

Richard tossed a triumphant gaze at Grady.

"Richard shows me magic tricks and dances with me.''

"Grady saved your life,'' Caroline reminded Maggie. After looking forward to this time with Grady all week, she wasn't about to let Richard ruin it.

Maggie's head drooped against Richard's chin and her arms circled his neck. "I still like Richard best.''

"Of course you do,'' Richard cooed. "All the women in this town do.''

"Except Ellie Frasier,'' Grady said in low tones.

The air between the two men crackled. Richard raised his eyebrows. "Well, well, so my brother knows how to score a point.''

"Caroline and Maggie came here to visit me.''

"If that's the way you want it,'' Richard said, and slowly set Maggie down. "I didn't realize they were your exclusive property. It's a shame because Caroline and I might have renewed an old acquaintance. We used to be good friends, remember?''

"We were never friends, Richard,'' she said, intensely disliking him.

"So that's the lay of the land, is it?'' Richard said, with a half smile that implied her words had wounded him. As though his heart was capable of entertaining anything other than selfish pursuits, she thought in disgust.

He walked away then, and despite everything, Caroline experienced a twinge of sadness. She regretted the waste of his skills, his potential. She'd known him all her life, but she didn't really *know* him. She didn't think anyone was capable of fully understanding Richard.

Grady reached for her hand. "I'm sorry, Caroline."

"It's fine. Don't worry about it."

Maggie didn't share her opinion, but Caroline wasn't concerned.

"Would you like some lemonade?" Grady asked her daughter. "I made it specially for you." He sounded downright pleased with himself.

"That sounds yummy, doesn't it?" Caroline said.

Maggie didn't answer.

"We'll take a glass," Caroline responded for both of them.

Grady led the way to the kitchen and got out three glasses. "It dawned on me the other day that I'm going to be living the bachelor life in a few months. I never spent much time in the kitchen, not with Mom around and then Savannah doing all the cooking." A sadness came over him at the mention of his mother. Grady wasn't one to openly display his emotions, but Caroline knew that the deaths of his parents had forever marked him. He never talked about the accident—they'd drowned in a flash flood—or the horrible weeks that followed with the discovery of Richard's theft and disappearance.

"I suspect Wiley and I'll starve to death before the end of the first month," he said, making a lighthearted shift of subject. Wiley had been foreman on the Yellow Rose for as long as Caroline could remember.

"I don't think Savannah will let that happen."

"Can I play with Savannah's dolls?" Maggie asked, tugging at her mother's arm.

"Don't you want to go riding?" Grady asked, sounding disappointed.

Maggie shook her head; Caroline supposed she'd been

scared off by the incident on Sunday. It might be a while before she was interested in horses again. In any event, dolls had always been her first choice.

"You be careful with Savannah's things, you hear?" Caroline warned.

"I will," Maggie promised, and skipped off, her lemonade untouched.

"She enjoys playing with dolls, doesn't she?" Grady said.

"More than anything."

Grady carried their lemonade into the living room and set both glasses down on the coffee table.

"I imagine you're wondering why we're sitting in here rather than outside," he said.

As a matter of fact she was.

"It's too damned difficult to find a way to hold you if you're sitting in that rocking chair," he confessed. "Damn it, woman, I haven't thought about anything but kissing you again from the moment you left last Sunday."

It was heaven to hear him say it, and hell to confess it herself. "Oh, Grady, me, too!"

Neither made a pretense of drinking the lemonade. The minute they were on the sofa, they were in each other's arms. Their first kiss was urgent, like a thirsty traveler drinking in cool water, not taking time to savor the taste or feel of it. Their second kiss was more serene.

Caroline wanted this, needed this, and Grady hadn't disappointed her. His own display of eagerness warmed her heart. A delightful excitement filled her, allowing her to hope, to dream.

"Is this really happening to us?" she asked. She shifted around and rested her back against his chest. He spread light kisses down the side of her neck.

"If it's not, don't wake me."

"When did this come about?" She closed her eyes and moaned softly when his teeth nipped her ear, sending shivers up her spine. "Grady," she groaned, half in protest, half in encouragement.

"Kiss me," he pleaded.

He didn't need to ask twice. She twisted around and offered him her mouth. The havoc his touch created within her was much too powerful to resist.

Caroline was too involved in their exchange to hear the door open.

Grady abruptly broke off the kiss. Stunned by the sudden change in him, she didn't notice Savannah for several seconds.

"Oops." Her best friend sounded infinitely cheerful. "I think we came back a little too soon, Laredo."

Chapter Six

"This is incredible!" Caroline cried, galloping after Grady. The wind blew in her face as her pinto followed Grady's horse across the wide open range. She hadn't gone horseback riding in ages, and it felt wonderful, exhilarating. Caroline couldn't remember a time she'd experienced such a sense of freedom. Not in years and years. This lighthearted feeling could only be attributed to one thing—the fact that she was falling in love with Grady.

"Come on, slowpoke," Grady shouted over his shoulder, leading her farther from the ranch house. He hadn't said where they were headed, but he seemed to have a destination in mind.

"Where are you taking me?" she called, but either he didn't hear or chose to ignore the question.

Bless Savannah's matchmaking heart. When she'd returned early, she insisted they go riding, saying she'd look after Maggie. Grady and Caroline had both made token protests, but it didn't take long for Savannah to convince them to sneak away.

The day was lovely, not excessively hot for an August afternoon. Surprisingly it was several degrees cooler than it had been earlier in the week. The grass was lush and green because of the early-summer rains, and the air smelled fresh.

During the last few days Caroline had been giving a lot of thought to her relationship with Grady. Both were mature adults. He'd recently turned thirty-six and she was almost twenty-eight. She knew what she wanted in life, and he seemed to have set his own course, too. She liked him and deeply respected him. Recently, very recently, she'd admitted she was fast falling in love with him. Already she was beginning to believe they could make a decent life together.

Grady crested a hill and stopped to wait for her. His eyes were bright, alive with happiness, and Caroline wondered if the joy she read in them was a reflection of her own.

"Are you ready for a break yet?" he asked.

"I'll rest when you do," she told him, not wanting to hold him up.

"In other words you're willing to follow me to the ends of the earth."

She laughed rather than confess the truth of it. "Something like that."

"Seriously, Caroline, my backside is far more accustomed to a saddle than yours. I don't want to overtax that part of your anatomy."

"I didn't know you were so concerned about the care and comfort of my butt," she teased.

Grady threw back his head and laughed boisterously.

She urged the pinto into an easy trot, and Grady caught up with her in short order. They rode in companionable silence for several minutes. Gradually he led her toward some willow trees growing along the edge of a winding creek. The scene was postcard picturesque.

"There's a nice shady spot here." Grady pointed to a huge weeping willow whose branches dipped lazily into the water.

They paused there. Grady dismounted first, then helped her down. Caroline had been around horses most of her life and certainly didn't need any assistance. But she didn't stop him; she knew he wanted to hold her, and she wanted it, too. She could find no reason to deny either of them what they desired.

He held her a moment longer than necessary and she pretended not to notice. Bracing her hands against his shoulders, she slowly eased her body toward the ground. Even then he didn't release his firm grasp on her waist.

His eyes were intense, focused only on her. Time seemed to stop. Everything around her had an unreal dreamlike quality. Sound filtered lazily into her mind—the whisper of a breeze through the delicate branches of the willow, the creek's cheerful gurgle, the bird song of early evening.

"I used to come here when I was a boy," Grady said. He still held her, but more loosely now. "I used to think it was a magic place."

"Magic?"

"Bandits hid in the tree, waiting to ambush me, but I was too smart for them." Laugh lines crinkled at his eyes as he spoke.

"When I was a little girl, I used to hide in an oak tree in our backyard. I was sure no one could see me."

He removed his glove and brushed a strand of hair from her temple, his callused fingers gentle against her face. "Once I'd rid the place of the bandits, I'd sit and think...and pretend."

"I'd dream," she told him, realizing as she did that this was the first time she'd ever told anyone about the oak tree.

"Any particular dream?" he asked.

"Oh, what most girls dream," she said. "Girls who've read *Cinderella* and *Rapunzel* and *Snow White*—I adored those stories. I'd dream about being a princess in disguise. A handsome prince would fight insurmountable odds to come to me and declare his love."

He grinned. "At your service."

"Oh, Grady, are you my prince?" She felt foolish when she'd said the words, but he looked at her so seriously, all joking gone.

"There's nothing I'd like more," he said in a quiet voice.

The air between them seemed electric, charged with tension, and Caroline was convinced she'd die if he didn't kiss her soon. Judging by the glitter in his eyes, Grady must have felt the same way. He muttered something unintelligible, then unhurriedly lowered his mouth to hers.

He tightened his arms around her waist, almost lifting her from the ground. Caroline ran her fingers through his hair. His Stetson tumbled from his head, but he didn't seem to notice. The kiss went on and on.

Abruptly he broke it off and shook his head. "I shouldn't have done that. I'm sorry. I'm moving too fast. It's just that—"

"No, that's not it."

His hands were in her hair, too, and he held her against him. With her ear pressed to his heart, she could hear its desperate pounding.

"I can't seem to keep my hands off you," he whispered.

"You don't hear me complaining, do you?"

"No, but…" His chest expanded with a deep sigh. "Oh, hell, Caroline, I haven't made any secret of the way I feel about you."

"It's how I feel, too," she confessed.

Holding her hand firmly in his, he guided her toward the creek, stopping long enough to retrieve a spare blanket from his saddlebag. He pulled back the dangling willow branches and bowed, gesturing her in. "Welcome to my castle."

"Castle?" she repeated. "I thought it was a bandits' hideout."

"Not anymore," he murmured. "I'm your handsome prince, remember?"

All Caroline could do was smile. And if her smile was a little tremulous…she couldn't help it.

He spread the blanket on the ground, and once she was seated, he returned to his saddlebag. To her surprise, he produced a bottle of cool white wine, two stemmed plastic glasses and a piece of cheddar cheese.

"You shock me, Grady," Caroline told him as he opened the bottle with his Swiss Army knife.

"I do?" He glanced up, a look of amusement on his face as he cut the cheese and handed her a slice.

"This is so *romantic*."

"If you think this is something, just wait."

Caroline raised her head. "You mean there's more?" She savoured a bite of the sharp cheddar.

"Much more." He leaped to his feet and returned to the horses. Again opening a saddlebag, he drew out a small gold-foil box.

"Chocolates?" Caroline squealed with delight.

"I figured these were the kind of thing a man gives a woman when he comes courting." He didn't look at her; instead, he busied himself carefully pouring the wine.

Caroline loved the way he used the old-fashioned term. "*Are* you courting me, Grady?" She'd meant to sound demure, but her question had an urgency about it. "Are you being serious?" She had to know.

"This is about as serious as a man gets," he said, and handed her a plastic cup of wine. "Shall we make a toast?" he asked, holding up his glass.

She nodded and touched her glass to his.

"To the future," he said, then amended, "Our future."

Caroline sipped the wine. The chardonnay was delicate, smooth, refreshing. One sip and her heart started to pound, the force of it growing with every beat. It took her a moment to realize what was happening.

She was in love, really in love. It both terrified and excited her. And with that realization came another. She needed to tell Grady about Maggie's father. He had a right to know the truth, although the thought of telling him brought a dull ache to the pit of her stomach.

"You're quiet all of a sudden," Grady said.

"I was just thinking." She shrugged off his concern.

"That could be dangerous to your mental health," he teased. He leaned forward, his lips moist with wine, and gently kissed her. His mouth lingered in a series of short nibbling kisses far more potent than the wine.

"I can't make myself stop kissing you," he said, leaning his forehead against hers.

"I can't stop wanting you to kiss me," she told him. She moved her hands along his neck, loving the feel of his skin. "I...I want to talk to you about Maggie." She closed her eyes, fighting back the tension that gripped her. The sooner she got this over with, the better.

"I'm trying, Caroline, I honestly am."

"I know...but what I want to say doesn't have anything to do with how she feels about you."

Grady went very still.

The heavy pounding of her heart echoed in her ears, drowning out her thoughts. She couldn't look at him while she spoke of that pain-filled time. Before she could stop herself, she was on her feet.

"It's about Maggie's father." She clenched her hands until the knuckles were white. Her stomach tightened. The only one who knew the full truth had been her mother. Caroline was well aware that other family members and certainly her friends had speculated for years about who'd fathered Maggie, but she'd never told them. Never told anyone. Never felt the need until now.

"Caroline, you're very pale. Is this really so difficult for you?"

She bowed her head and exhaled slowly. "It's much harder than I'd thought it would be."

He stood up and moved behind her, placing his hands on her shoulders. "Then forget it. My knowing isn't necessary, not if it upsets you like this."

"But it *is* necessary." He had no idea how much.

"Then you can tell me some other time," he insisted. He bent to kiss the side of her neck. His mouth lingered and her head fell forward. "I want our afternoon to be special. I don't want anything to interfere with that."

"But you have a right to know." She paused and swallowed. What he didn't seem to understand was that telling him wouldn't get any easier. In fact, the longer she waited...

His hands gently stroked the length of her arms. "Let's not spoil our afternoon with memories best forgotten. There'll be plenty of time for you to tell me everything—but not today."

"Aren't you curious? Don't you want to know?"

He released a long sigh. "Yeah, I am," he said after a moment. "Perhaps I'm a little afraid, too. I don't want anything to ruin what we have."

"Oh, Grady." He made it so easy to delay telling him the truth. Easy to thrust it into the future with excuses she was far too willing to accept and he was just as eager to suggest.

"I'm your prince, remember?"

"I remember," she replied dutifully.

"Good." He kissed her then, his mouth touching hers in a quick caress. "Now let's get back to our wine."

He waited until she'd settled herself on the blanket before he handed her the glass he'd refilled. Positioning himself behind her, he eased her against him. Caroline closed her eyes as he gently fingered the fine strands of her hair.

"I told you this is a magic place."

"Mmm."

"Reality will find us soon enough, so let's enjoy the magic while we can."

Caroline had to admit she was willing to do just that.

MAGGIE PUT Savannah's dolls back on the bedroom-window seat and looked out again, hoping to see her mommy. She'd gone horseback riding with Grady and they'd been away a long time. Longer than she wanted them to be. She was ready to go home now.

Bored, she put on her backpack and wandered into the kitchen where Savannah was kneading bread dough.

"When's Mommy coming back?" she asked.

"I don't know, sweetheart, but I imagine they'll be here soon."

"Where's Richard?" Maggie asked next.

"I don't know."

"Can I watch television?"

"Of course, but get Laredo to turn it on for you, okay?"

"I can do it," Maggie insisted. She turned on the television at home and it wasn't hard.

"Grady got a new satellite dish and it has three remote controls."

There was his name again. Not only did Grady shout, but he made it so she couldn't prove to Savannah how smart she was.

"Laredo's in the barn, but he'll be finished any minute."

Maggie glanced wistfully toward the barn, but she wouldn't go in there alone, not anymore. The last time, she'd gotten into trouble, and Grady had yelled at her again and grabbed her. He'd been scared, too; she could tell when he pulled her away from the horse and held her.

"I'd do it for you, sweetheart, but I've got my hands buried in bread dough." Savannah explained.

"That's all right." Not wanting to wait inside, Maggie

walked onto the porch. She sat on the top step, and Rocket ambled over to lie down beside her. She rubbed his ears for a few minutes because Savannah had told her he liked that. Then she rested her chin on her folded hands, looking out over the ranch yard, hoping she'd find something to do. Something that wouldn't get her in trouble.

She caught a flash of color and saw Richard coming out of the bunk house. Her spirits lifted immediately. Leaping off the steps, she raced to his side. "Richard!"

He jerked around, then smiled when he saw her. Maggie liked Richard's smile, but what she enjoyed most were his magic tricks. Once he pulled a coin out of her ear. Another time he had her draw a card out of the middle of a deck and then told her what card it was. He was right.

"Howdy, kiddo," Richard said.

"Wanna play?" she asked, skipping after him.

"Not now."

"Nobody wants to play with me," she said, hoping he'd feel sorry for her and offer a game or a few tricks.

"Sorry, kiddo, I've got things to do."

Maggie's face fell. Everyone was too busy for her. "Can I help?" she asked, thinking if he finished early, he might take time to play.

No," he said sharply. He sounded almost like Grady when he was mad, and Maggie gasped.

Richard squatted down. "Maybe we can play, after all. How about a game of hide-and-seek?" he suggested. "You go hide and I'll come and find you."

This was great, better than she'd expected. "Okay." Maggie glanced around, looking for a place to hide, somewhere Richard wouldn't find her.

"Are you closing your eyes?" she asked.

"You bet I am, kid."

Maggie didn't like the way he said it, but she was so

pleased to have someone willing to play with her that she didn't care.

"Don't peek," she warned, and raced around the corner.

"I wouldn't dream of it," he called after her.

He said that in a way she didn't like, either. Almost as if he was mad but without raising his voice. Maggie tore across the yard, her pack slapping against her back, and hid in Savannah's garden. She liked the smell of the roses. She crouched down under the table on the patio…but Richard didn't come and he didn't come. She got tired of waiting.

He was probably looking in places near the barn, she decided. Sneaking out of the rose garden, she crept on tiptoe closer to where she'd last seen him. Circling around to the other side of the barn, she saw Grady's truck that Richard sometimes drove. He didn't usually keep his truck there. The truck bed was covered with a sort of blanket but bigger.

Richard would never think of looking for her there. The tailgate was down, and by standing on a box she was able to climb inside. The floor hurt her knees and it was dark and warm inside, almost like a cave under the heavy cloth. There was lots of other stuff, too. She found a rolled-up sleeping bag and leaned against it.

"Richard!" she called, thinking he might need help finding her.

Nothing.

It was getting so hot under the blanket that she took off the backpack. Soon her eyes grew heavy with sleep. She decided to put her head down on the sleeping bag, but just for a few minutes until Richard found her.

Just until then.

THIS WAS SO EASY it was embarrassing, Richard Weston told himself. The pickup, formerly owned by Grady—as he liked to think of it—sped down the road toward Bitter End.

No one would think of looking for him there. No one would even guess.

Luckily his brother's head was in the clouds these days. Grady Weston in love—if it wasn't so damn funny, it'd be sad. Grady had fallen in love—for the first time, Richard was sure—at the age of thirty-six—and it wasn't a pretty sight. For a couple of weeks now he'd been walking around the house with his tongue hanging out of his mouth and his eyes glazed over. It was a wonder he hadn't tripped down the stairs and broken his damn neck.

Actually Richard wouldn't have minded doing the dirty deed with Miss Caroline himself. He'd bet that woman was some hot number in the sack. Still, he felt grateful to her for keeping Grady distracted. His blockhead of a brother didn't have a clue what he, Richard, was up to. Before Grady figured it out, he'd be long gone. Yup, it was that easy.

Richard laughed aloud. "Idiots." He hated to say this about his own flesh and blood, but both Grady and Savannah were dolts. It was kind of sad that they'd be gullible enough to let him drive off with several months' worth of supplies. He'd even managed to acquire a small gasoline-powered generator—one he'd put onto his brother's business account, naturally. Of course Grady wouldn't know anything about it for a couple of weeks.

Richard almost wished he could be a fly on the wall when the bills started coming in. Grady would have a conniption. Richard felt a mild twinge of guilt about that, but hell, he didn't have any choice. Not really. He had to eat, and while the portable television might seem an extravagance, it wasn't. How would he know what was going on in the world without watching the evening news? It wasn't like he was going to get cable in the old ghost town, either. All he had were rabbit ears. He'd be lucky to receive one station, possibly two, but that was probably just as well.

Otherwise he'd be tempted to laze around and waste his whole supply of gasoline on running the TV.

By the time he reached the turnoff to the dirt road that wound up the far side of the valley, he was lost in his thoughts.

He knew himself well enough to realize he'd find it difficult to stay cooped up in Bitter End, with no companionship and few diversions. There were sure to be times when he'd welcome an excuse to venture into Promise, or any one of the other small towns that dotted the Texas hill country.

He couldn't do that, however. Grady was bound to report the truck as stolen, and sure as shootin', Richard would have a lawman on his tail five minutes after he hit the highway. But a stolen vehicle was only a small part of Richard's worries—just one more complication in his already complicated life.

Hell, all the lawmen in three states would give their eyeteeth to get their hands on him. So the last thing he needed was to be pulled in for driving a stolen truck.

A shiver raced down his spine. He didn't want to think about that.

The road grew bumpy and he slowed. For a moment he thought he heard a sound, a cry of some kind, but he strained his ears and didn't hear it again.

Imagination was a funny thing, he mused. Could be dangerous, too. On a recent visit to Bitter End, he'd had the impression that someone was watching him. Someone or something. A vague feeling, mildly uncomfortable.

He blamed Ellie Frasier for that. She'd given him the willies the time he'd brought her to Bitter End. The minute they left the truck, she'd started making noises about this "feeling." He hadn't felt a damn thing, while she was practically crawling out of her skin. Naturally that was for the best, since he certainly didn't want her coming back and bringing her friends along.

Ellie hadn't been able to get out fast enough. Whatever the feeling was, it had never bothered Richard—until that last visit. He'd probably just heard too much about this so-called sensation. He didn't understand it, but he was counting it as a plus. The town's reputation for eeriness meant that people would stay away. He'd have to control his own imagination, not let ghost stories and strange noises spook him.

As he neared Bitter End, he reduced the truck's speed. He'd found a spot in the ghost town where he could hide the pickup, so if anyone did happen to stumble in, they wouldn't see it.

He stopped in front of the wooden stable, which leaned heavily to one side. He'd say one thing for the folks who'd originally built this place. They'd been great craftsmen. Most of the buildings still stood, despite their age.

He drove the truck into the decrepit stable and jumped down from the cab. He was about to close the door when he caught a movement under the canvas tarp.

He froze. Sure enough, he saw it move again. Believing in the element of surprise, he moved quietly to the back of the truck and firmly gripped the edge of the blanket. With no warning, he jerked it away from the bed.

Maggie Daniels screamed and cowered in a corner. It took them both a moment to recover, but she was faster.

"Richard!"

"What the hell are you doing here?" he demanded.

The smile on her face disappeared. "We were playing hide-and-seek, remember? I fell asleep...."

Richard swore.

Maggie's eyes grew round. "If my mommy was here, she'd wash your mouth out with soap."

As far as he could see, Richard had few choices. He

could dump the kid on the highway—but would she shut up about where she'd been? He could keep her in Bitter End. Or he could do away with her entirely. Kidnap and murder charges wouldn't look good on his rap sheet. But he might not have any other options.

Damn it, what was he going to do now?

GRADY HAD NEVER been one to idle away time, nor had he been known to sit under a willow tree and soak in the beauty of a summer evening. Not for the past six years, at any rate. It'd taken him that long to get the ranch into the black. He'd earned a decent profit last year and would again this year, God willing. He finally felt good about his life and he didn't want his happiness compromised now with talk of Maggie's father. He tried to tell himself it didn't matter—but it did. Caroline had wanted to tell him, and curious though he was, he'd persuaded her to wait. Grady recognized that his be-havior was uncharacteristic; generally he faced problems head-on. But he knew why he didn't want to hear what she had to say. Admitting it didn't come easy, not by a long shot. Intuitively he feared that once she told him about Maggie's father, nothing would be the same between them. Sitting with her in the shade of the willow tree, holding her close, loving her—these moments were far too special to invade with difficult truths. So he'd delayed the inevitable, hurled it into the future until he felt more ready to deal with it.

Caroline lay down on the blanket beside him, her head resting against his thigh. Lazily he brushed the hair from her face. She was so damned beautiful he could barely manage not to stare at her. Barely manage not to kiss her again. They'd done plenty of that this afternoon. She'd tasted of wine and chocolate, and Grady thought he'd never sampled a more intoxicating combination. Sweet and potent at the same time.

He'd as good as told her he was interested in marrying her. A man didn't go courting otherwise. It was time for him to settle down. Glen was about to make the leap into marriage, and with Savannah married and she and Laredo building their own home, he'd soon be alone. But it wasn't just the events in other people's lives that had convinced him.

It was Caroline and Maggie. Whenever he was with them, he didn't want their time together to end. His life felt empty when they weren't around.

He tried to tell Caroline that, but he couldn't manage the words. He discovered it was damned hard to admit how much he needed someone else. He'd never felt this way before, and it frightened him.

"I could almost go to sleep," Caroline murmured. Her eyes remained closed and he ran his index finger down the side of her jaw. Her skin was soft and smooth. Lovely. *She* was lovely.

Her lips eased into a smile. "You're right."

"Well, I don't know what I'm right about, but I like the sound of those words."

"Every man does," she teased.

"Flatter my ego and tell me why I'm right."

"This place," she whispered. "I don't think I've ever felt so…content. So relaxed."

"Me neither." Today was the first time he'd spent more than ten minutes here in years, and already they'd been gone at least two hours.

"I wonder…" she began wistfully.

"What?" He bent forward to graze his lips across her brow.

"If you have any other magic tricks up your sleeve."

"That's Richard's specialty, not mine."

Caroline frowned. "You provided a magical afternoon

for me,'' she said. ''Wine and chocolates and this beautiful place.''

''The kissing wasn't half-bad, either.''

Her eyes fluttered open and she gazed up at him with such longing he couldn't possibly have resisted her.

Caroline wrapped herself in his embrace the moment he reached for her. Grady was shocked by the intensity of his own craving. It felt as though he'd waited his entire life for this afternoon and this woman.

His tongue danced with hers and he worked his fingers into her hair, loving the feel of it, clean and silky smooth. Fifty years of this, and he swore he'd never tire of her taste.

''I suppose we'd better think about getting back,'' he said reluctantly, feeling cheated that their magical time had come to an end.

''How long have we been gone?'' Caroline asked. Not waiting for a response, she glanced at her watch. She gasped and jumped to her feet. ''Oh, my goodness, we've been away for over two hours!''

''I know.''

''But Maggie...''

''She's with Savannah.''

''I had no idea we'd been gone this long.'' She started cleaning up the area, her movements fast and jerky.

''Caroline, you don't have anything to worry about.''

She turned slowly to face him, obviously comforted. ''Thank you Grady. I do know that. I'm just not used to...any of *this*.'' She made a gesture that took in their surroundings, the remains of their picnic and Grady himself.

He helped her mount—because he wanted to, not because she needed any assistance. They rode back to the ranch, joking and laughing, teasing each other the way lovers do.

As the house came into view, his eyes were drawn to its

silhouette against the darkening sky. Solid, secure, welcoming. His home had always seemed a natural part of the landscape to him. It belonged there. And for the first time in years, he felt that his life was what he wanted it to be.

It wasn't until they neared the corral that Grady noticed something was amiss. He saw Laredo, and the minute the other man caught sight of Grady and Caroline, he ran into the house, calling for Savannah. She rushed out onto the back porch.

His sister's face was red, her eyes puffy as though she'd been weeping. That wasn't like her.

"What is it?" he asked as he dismounted.

"Oh, Caroline, I'm so sorry." Savannah's voice trembled and she covered her mouth.

Confused, Caroline looked to Grady. "What's wrong?"

Grady walked around his gelding and helped Caroline down from her horse. Her hands trembled as she held his arms.

"Where's Maggie?" she asked, her voice oddly calm.

"That's the problem," Laredo said, moving to stand next to his wife. He slid his arm around Savannah's shoulders.

"You don't know where Maggie is?" Caroline asked, and again Grady heard that strange calm in her voice.

"I... She went outside, and the last time I checked she was sitting on the porch," Savannah cried. "I've looked everywhere, called for her until my voice was hoarse. I don't know where she could have gone."

"Apparently she'd come out to look for me," Laredo said.

"Did you see her?" Grady demanded.

"No." Laredo shook his head.

"Oh, Caroline," Savannah wept, "I'm so sorry! I should never have let her leave the house."

Caroline's fingers dug into Grady's arm. Her eyes were

Chapter Seven

The calls lawmen dreaded most were domestic violence and missing children. Frank Hennessey was no exception. The report of a missing child made his blood run cold. He preferred dealing with a drunken belligerent husband any day of the week if it meant he didn't have to see the face of a parent whose child couldn't be found. Frank had never married, never had children, but he'd been a firsthand witness to the agony parents endure when their child disappears. All his years of law enforcement had convinced him there was no deeper pain than the loss of a child.

The call that Maggie Daniels had gone missing came minutes before Frank was due to go off duty. Grady Weston phoned it in. There'd only been one other time Frank had heard Grady sound the way he did this evening, and that was the day his parents had drowned in a flash flood.

"Are you sure she hasn't fallen asleep somewhere in the house?" Frank felt obliged to ask.

"We're sure, Frank." Grady's impatience crackled over the telephone line.

"Was she upset about anything?"

"No, she was excited about visiting the ranch," Caroline answered, apparently from one of the extensions.

"Maggie didn't run away, if that's what you're thinking," Grady told him angrily.

In fact, Frank's questions had been leading to that assumption. It was the most common scenario, even with kids this young. He sighed heavily. He hadn't been around children much, but he'd taken a real liking to Caroline's fatherless child. She was a sweetheart, and the thought of anything happening to her made his insides twist.

"Are you coming out to take a report or not?" Grady demanded.

"I'm on my way." Frank replaced the receiver. Grady sounded as worried and frustrated as he would if he were the child's father. In situations such as this the families were often impatient and angry, lashing out at authority because of their own helplessness. Frank had seen it before. Some of the cases he'd worked on came with happy endings. The lost child was found safe and promptly returned to the parents.

The other cases, two in his career, would forever haunt him. *Missing*. He'd come to think of it as the ugliest word in the English language. The first child had turned up dead; the second was never seen again.

Although the highway was deserted, Frank ran the lights on his patrol car as he sped toward the Yellow Rose Ranch. The entire forty minutes it took him to drive from town, he kept hoping against hope that by the time he arrived, Maggie would've been found. He wasn't a superstitious man, nor did he believe in intuition, but his gut told him that wouldn't be the case.

He was right.

No sooner had he pulled into the yard than the door opened and Grady hurried onto the porch. Caroline was with him, looking paler than he'd ever seen her. Grady's eyes were dark with anxiety.

"Thank you for coming," Caroline said, her voice determined. She was a strong woman and Frank deeply admired her grit.

Grady held the door open for him. "Savannah's got coffee brewing," he said, leading the way into the kitchen.

Frank looked around at the small group assembled there. Laredo had his arm around Savannah, who seemed on the verge of collapse. Her eyes were red and swollen, testifying to the tears she'd already shed.

"It's my fault," she said.

"No one's laying blame," Grady told her, his eyes softening. He brought the coffeepot over to the table where a number of mugs had been set, and he filled each one.

"But I was supposed to be watching her," Savannah explained as Frank doctored his coffee with milk.

"It doesn't matter who was watching her," Caroline said, her voice shaking slightly. "What matters is that we don't know where Maggie is now."

"We'll find her," Wiley Rogers, the foreman, insisted. "Don't you worry about that. Not a one of us will rest until Maggie's found."

Frank had heard words like that before, and he'd watched as families invested every penny of their life's savings in the effort. He'd watched them invest the very heart and soul of their existence in tracing a missing child, sometimes to the point that the entire family was destroyed. He'd assumed when he moved to Promise fifteen years ago that he'd never have to deal with this sort of agony again, but he'd been wrong. It was staring him in the face this very minute.

"Savannah, since you were the last person to see Maggie, why don't we start with you." He withdrew a small notebook from his shirt pocket. "You *were* the last one to see her, right?"

Savannah nodded and Laredo moved closer to his wife's side as if to protect her. Frank pitied her, understood the grief and guilt she must feel. He glanced away and surveyed everyone else in the room.

It was then that he noticed one family member was missing. "Where's Richard?" he asked, interrupting Savannah.

"In town, I suspect," Grady said.

"Driving what?"

"My pickup's missing, so I guess he has that."

Frank walked over to the telephone. "I want him here."

"Of course," Savannah said.

"You don't think he'd take Maggie with him, do you?" Caroline asked, looking to Grady and Savannah for the answer. "I mean, we assumed he left earlier, before Maggie turned up missing, but…" She let the rest fade.

"It isn't a good idea to assume anything." Frank walked over to the wall phone and lifted the receiver. He barked out a few orders, then instructed his deputy to drive through town and find Richard Weston. If Richard wasn't there, Al was to find out the last time anyone saw him and report back to Frank as soon as possible.

While he waited for Al to return the call, Frank finished the interview with Savannah and Laredo. An hour passed before the phone rang. Caroline leaped from her chair and her eyes grew wide and hopeful when Grady reached for the receiver. Without a word he handed the telephone to Frank.

Richard Weston was nowhere to be found. Neither was Grady's truck. No one had seen him, not that day or the day before. Al reported that he wasn't the only one looking for Richard, either, but Frank decided these people had enough trouble on their hands. He didn't intend to add to it.

"You don't honestly think Richard took the child, do you?" Savannah asked after he'd relayed the details of Al's findings.

"At this point I won't discount any coincidence. Maggie's missing and so is Richard."

"But I'm sure he left long before Maggie disappeared," Savannah said.

"I'm not." This came from Laredo. "I saw the truck. And I saw it while Maggie was in the house with you."

UNABLE TO SLEEP, Caroline sat on the dark porch, her arms wrapped protectively around her middle. Frank had left several hours earlier. There was nothing more he could do; he'd already alerted law-enforcement officers across Texas and in the adjoining states to keep their eyes open for Maggie. Savannah had given the sheriff Maggie's school photograph and he'd taken it into town with him. Soon Maggie's likeness would be seen in every law office in the Southwest. The search was on for Richard, too, with an all points bulletin issued for his arrest. Caroline knew that had something to do with information the sheriff had received, information about a crime Richard had committed back East. She didn't know what it was, and right now she didn't care. Finding Maggie was the only thing that mattered.

With nothing further to be done at the moment, everyone had turned in for the night. Frank had offered to follow her home, but Caroline refused to leave. If Maggie—she paused and rephrased the thought—*when* Maggie came back, Caroline wanted to be right here at the ranch waiting for her.

Although everyone had gone to bed, she knew no one would sleep well. She accepted one of Savannah's nightgowns and made the pretense of going to bed, too, but the room felt suffocating. Within minutes she'd dressed again and made her way through the house and outside. She sat on the porch steps and stared into the bleak darkness.

It wasn't long before Grady joined her. Wordlessly, with barely a sound, he sat down on the step next to her and clasped her hand. Her fingers tightened around his.

"I'm so afraid." It was the first time she'd verbalized her fears.

"I am, too."

She pressed her head against his shoulder and he placed his arm around her, drawing her close.

"Do you think she's with Richard?" Caroline couldn't shake the thought. They'd both disappeared around the same time, but that made no sense. Richard might be a lot of things, but a child-snatcher wasn't one of them. Caroline could think of no plausible reason for him to take Maggie.

"I can't imagine that even Richard would do anything like this," Grady said, his voice little more than a whisper.

Caroline reminded herself that Frank believed there might be a connection between Maggie's disappearance and Richard's. She just couldn't understand what it might be.

"You should try to sleep," Grady urged.

"I can't." Every time she closed her eyes her imagination tormented her. She couldn't bear the thought of her daughter hurt and crying out for her. But that was what filled her mind and heart and made sleep impossible.

"I can't, either."

"Oh, Grady," she whispered, her voice breaking. "Where can she be?"

He waited a moment before he answered, and she knew he was experiencing the same frustration she was. "I wish I knew."

As the night wore on, it became more and more difficult for Caroline to hope. When she couldn't stand the silence any longer, she buried her face in her hands and cried, "I want my daughter!"

She tried to be strong, but she didn't think she could hold back the tears. Hysteria was edging in on her. She could feel it pushing her closer to the brink.

All at once she was completely wrapped in Grady's

arms. She clung to him, shaking almost uncontrollably as she muffled her sobs against his chest. His hold on her was firm, solid, and she needed him as she'd rarely needed anyone in her life. She wept until there were no tears left.

"This might be the worst possible time to tell you this," Grady whispered, his mouth close to her ear. "I love you, Caroline."

"Oh, Grady," she sobbed.

"I know it's new, and it might take some getting used to, but let my love be your strength for now. Lean on me if you can. Let me help you bear this. I'll do everything in my power to get Maggie back."

She was holding him, clutching his shoulders, like a lifeline. "I love you, too," she whimpered, but didn't know if he'd heard her.

"We'll get through this," he promised. "We'll find Maggie."

He sounded confident and sure, and she clung to the promise of his words.

"It's going to be all right, understand?"

She nodded, desperately wanting to believe him.

Oh, God, she prayed, *please bring my little girl home.*

But God seemed far away just then.

MAGGIE'S EYES were sore from crying, but she didn't want Richard to hear her because he'd already gotten mad and yelled at her. She huddled in the corner of the old stone building that used to be a store. It was getting dark, but there was still some light coming in through the open door. Richard had told her not to leave the room and then he'd disappeared. Maggie didn't like Richard anymore, even if he *could* do magic tricks.

He was mean and he said bad words and he threw things, too. After he found her hiding in the back of Grady's pickup, he started acting like Billy Parsons when he had a temper tantrum at his brother's birthday party. The only thing Richard didn't do was throw himself down on the ground and start kicking.

Her stomach growled, but Maggie had already looked around for something to eat and hadn't found anything. She wished she'd gone horseback riding with her mommy and Grady. She was afraid of horses after last Sunday—but not nearly as afraid as she was now.

"Richard," Maggie said, risking his wrath by walking out of the store. "I want to go home now, okay?"

"Yeah, well, you can't have everything you want." He was sitting outside and he had a big bottle in his hand. Every now and then, he'd take a drink. Her mother had told Maggie it wasn't good manners to drink out of a bottle, but she didn't tell Richard that because he'd only yell at her again.

"Can we go back to the ranch?" she asked.

"No." He growled the word at her and laughed when she leaped back, frightened by the harsh sound of his voice. "I've got an idea," he said, leaning toward her. "Why don't you go fall in an empty well and save me a lot of trouble?"

Maggie hurried back into the old store and sat down on the lone chair. When it grew dark, she ventured over to the stable where he'd parked the truck. There was enough moonlight to find her way, but she walked very carefully, afraid of holes in the road and snakes…and Richard. Climbing into the bed of the pickup, she curled up with the sleeping bag she'd found earlier. She was cold and hungry and more afraid than she'd ever been in her whole life.

Every once in a while she could hear Richard singing. He played his guitar and sang, but his voice didn't sound right. It was like he'd mashed all the words together. She used to think he had a good voice; she didn't think so anymore.

Soon she fell asleep and didn't awake till light peeked through a crack in the stable door. She was so hungry her stomach hurt.

She clambered out of the truck and walked back to the main street. The early morning was very still.

Richard was asleep in the rocker. His guitar lay on the wooden sidewalk beside him, and he'd slouched down in the chair with his feet stretched out. His arms dangled over the edges of the rocker until his fingertips touched the ground close to the empty bottle. His head lolled to one side.

"Richard," she whispered. "I'm hungry."

He opened his eyes and blinked a couple of times.

"I'm hungry," she repeated, louder this time.

"Get out of here, kid."

"I want my mommy," she said, and her lower lip wobbled. "I don't like it here. I want to go home."

Richard slowly sat up and rubbed his face. "Get lost, will ya?"

Maggie didn't mean to, but she started to cry. She'd always thought Richard was her friend, and now she knew he wasn't.

"Stop it!" he shouted, and scowled at her.

Sobbing, Maggie ran away from him.

"Maggie," he called after her, but she didn't stop, running between two of the buildings.

"Damn it."

Maggie pretended not to hear him and, thinking he might try to follow her, she crept down the side of a building, then slipped inside another store.

The town was old. Really, really old. Older than any place she'd ever been. It smelled old. None of the buildings had paint, either. It sure seemed like no one had lived here for a long time. Some of the places had stuff inside. The store had a table and chair and shelves. But there were only a few cans sitting around—they looked kind of strange, like they might burst. Plus a cash register. She'd tried to get it to work, but it wouldn't open for her.

Maggie wasn't sure what kind of shop this had been, but it had a big cupboard. Maybe she could hide from Richard there. She opened the door and saw that it had shelves. On one of the shelves was a doll. A really old one, with a cotton dress and apron and bonnet. The doll's face had been stitched on. It wasn't like any doll she'd ever seen. The only one she owned with cloth arms and legs was Raggedy Ann, but her clothes were bright and pretty. This doll's clothes were all faded.

"Are you scared, too?" she asked the doll.

The stitched red mouth seemed to quaver a bit.

Suddenly she heard Richard's footsteps outside.

"Maggie, damn it! You could get hurt racing around this old town."

Maggie didn't care what Richard said—she didn't like him. She crouched down inside the cupboard and shut the door, leaving it open just a crack so she could see out.

"Are you hungry?" he called. She watched him stop in the doorway, staring into the building. Maggie's heart pounded hard and she bit her lower lip, afraid he might see her.

"Come on, kid," he growled.

Maggie clutched the old doll to her chest and closed her eyes. She wanted Richard to go away.

"I'm going to cook breakfast now," he said, moving away. He continued down the sidewalk with heavy footsteps. "When you're ready, you can come and eat, too."

Maggie waited a long time and didn't move until she smelled bacon frying. Her stomach growled again. The bacon smelled so good. It'd been hours and hours since she'd eaten.

Her grip on the doll loosened and she looked into its face

again. It was a sad face, Maggie realized, as if the doll was about to cry. Maggie felt like crying, too. She missed her mommy.

Slipping her backpack off her shoulders, Maggie opened it and carefully tucked the sad doll inside.

"I cooked you some bacon and eggs," Richard called.

This time Maggie couldn't resist. She pushed open the cupboard door and slowly walked out of the old building.

"There you are," Richard said, holding out a plate to her.

Maggie didn't trust Richard anymore and moved cautiously toward him. If he said something mean, she was prepared to run.

"I'm sorry I yelled at you," Richard told her.

"What about the bad words?"

"I'm sorry about those, too."

"Will you take me home now?" she asked, standing in the middle of the dirt street.

Richard stood by the post where people used to hitch their horses. He didn't look like he was sorry, even if he said he was.

Maggie's stomach was empty and making funny noises.

"You really want to go home now?" Richard asked. He sounded surprised that she'd want to leave. He made it seem like she was supposed to be having fun.

"I want to see my mommy."

"Okay, okay, but we need to talk about it first." He set the plate of food aside and sat down on the steps leading to the raised sidewalk.

"Why?"

He scratched his head. "Do you remember Grady getting mad at Savannah about coming to the ghost town?" he asked.

Maggie nodded. Grady had been real upset with Savannah when he found out she'd been to the town. Savannah had come to look for special roses, and Grady had stomped around the house for days. Even Laredo wasn't happy when Savannah wanted to come back and look for more roses.

"Now, this is very important," Richard said, his voice low and serious. "You mustn't let anyone know where you've been, understand?"

Her chin came up a little. "Why not?"

"You love your mommy, don't you?"

Maggie nodded.

"If anyone finds out you've been here..." He stopped and glanced in both directions as if he was afraid someone might be listening. "If anyone finds out, then something really bad will happen to your mother."

Maggie's eyes grew big.

"Do you know what ghosts are?" Richard asked.

"Melissa Washington dressed up in a sheet and said she was a ghost last Halloween," Maggie told him.

"There are good ghosts and bad ghosts."

"Which kind live here?" Maggie whispered.

"Bad ones," he whispered back. His voice was spooky. She wondered if he was trying to scare her on purpose.

"Bad ones?" she repeated, faintly.

"Very bad ones, and if you tell anyone, even your best friend, then the bad ghosts will find out and hurt your mother."

"How...how will they hurt Mommy?"

"You don't want to know, kid." He squeezed his eyes shut and made an ugly face, as if just telling her about it would upset him.

Maggie blinked, not sure she should believe him.

"Remember when Wiley cut his hand and Savannah had to wrap it up for him?"

"Yes..."

"That's what bad ghosts will do to your mommy, only it wouldn't just be her hand."

Maggie forgot all about the smell of bacon. Wiley's hand had bled and bled. Blood had gotten everywhere, and she could remember being surprised that one hand had so much blood in it. Just looking at it had made her feel sick to her stomach.

"You wouldn't want anything bad like that to happen to your mommy, would you?"

Maggie shook her head.

"I didn't think so."

"Can I go home now?"

He studied her for a long time. "You won't tell anyone?"

"No."

"Cross your heart?"

"Cross my heart." She made a big X over her heart.

"I'd hate to see your Mommy hurt, wouldn't you?"

Maggie nodded.

"Then maybe it'd be all right if I took you home."

Maggie sighed with relief. She was tired and hungry, and all she wanted was to see her mother again.

Richard helped her into the cab of Grady's truck. He made her curl up on the seat and keep her head down so she couldn't see as they drove away. Every time she closed her eyes she thought about a bad ghost and what might happen to her mother if she told anyone where she'd been. She still wasn't sure if Richard was lying, but she couldn't take any chances. She remembered how angry Grady had been with Savannah. When she asked her mother about it, Caroline had explained that Savannah had gone to a dangerous place. Now Maggie understood why Grady was so upset. That town was really creepy, and the more she thought about it, the more she believed there were bad things in those buildings.

The ride was bumpy and she was tossed about, but Richard wouldn't let her sit up and look out the window until they were on the real road.

"Remember, kid, you never saw me. Got that?"

"I never saw you," she repeated solemnly.

"Your mother's life depends on you keeping your trap shut. You wouldn't want your mother dead, would you?"

"No."

"Good. Just remember that the first time you're tempted to tell someone where you were."

"I'll remember. I won't tell." Maggie didn't want her mommy to die. Not like her grandmother. Or Savannah's parents. Or Emma Bishop's daddy.

Richard didn't drive her all the way back to the Yellow Rose. He stopped at the top of the driveway, leaned across her and opened the truck door.

"Remember what I said," he told her again. His eyes were mean.

"I'll remember," she promised, and before he could change his mind, she climbed out of the truck. She stumbled as she jumped down and fell, scraping her elbows. She began to cry, hardly noticing that Richard had driven off, tires squealing.

With her backpack hitting her shoulder blades, Maggie raced toward the ranch house. The driveway was long and her legs felt like they were on fire before the house finally came into view.

Grady stood on the porch with a cup of coffee, but the moment he saw her, he gave a loud shout and flung the cup away. Then he leaped off the porch without using any of the steps and ran toward her.

Almost immediately afterward, her mother threw open the screen door and placed both hands over her mouth. Then she started running, too. Maggie had never been so happy to see her mother. She was even glad to see Grady.

He waited for Caroline and let her go to Maggie first. Maggie liked that.

Her mother caught her in her arms and held her tight, then started to cry. She was worried about the bad ghosts, Maggie reasoned. She didn't need to be afraid, because Maggie wouldn't tell. Not anyone. Not ever.

Grady wrapped his arms around them both. He closed his eyes the way people did in church when they prayed. When he opened them again, he smiled at her. Maggie liked the way he smiled. It was a nice smile, not mean.

"Boy, we're glad to see you," he said.

SAVANNAH WIPED the tears from her face as she strolled along the pathway in her rose garden. But this morning she didn't appreciate the beauty of the roses. Nor did she find the solace she normally did here. If she lived to be a hundred years old, she didn't want to go through another day like the past one.

Although Caroline had repeatedly told her it wasn't her fault that Maggie had turned up missing, Savannah blamed herself. She'd been preoccupied with baking bread, her head full of the romance developing between her brother and her best friend. What she *should* have been doing was keeping careful watch over her best friend's child.

"I thought I'd find you here." Laredo walked up from behind her.

She didn't want him to know she'd been crying, but wasn't sure she could hide it.

"Sweetheart, why are you still upset? Maggie's home safe and sound."

"I know."

"Then what's bothering you?"

Her chest tightened, and she waited until the ache eased before she answered. "My brother."

Laredo clasped her shoulders. "Richard?"

She nodded. "He was involved in Maggie's disappearance. I know it."

"I have to admit it's mighty suspicious."

"Maggie won't say a word. Everyone's tried to get her to say where she was, but she refuses. Even Frank Hennessey can't get her to budge."

"It doesn't matter. She's home now."

"But it *does* matter," Savannah said passionately. "Laredo, tell me, where did Grady and I go wrong?"

"Sweetheart, your brother's an adult who makes his own decisions. You didn't do anything wrong. You're his sister, not his mother, and even if you were, I'd say the same thing. Richard is his own person, responsible for himself."

"In my head I agree with everything you're saying, but that doesn't take away the pain."

Laredo guided her to the patio set and made her sit down in one of the white wrought-iron chairs.

"I was the one who convinced Grady to let him stay."

"Yes, but that's because Richard's your brother."

"If I'd listened to Grady that first night, none of this would have happened."

"Oh, my love, that's the risk of having a gentle heart. Someone's bound to take advantage of it. I'm sorry it had to be your own brother."

"He's hurt so many people." That was what troubled Savannah most. It wasn't just she and Grady who'd been hurt, but others. Who knew how many? Wherever he'd spent the past six years, she had no doubt he'd left victims behind. People like the shopkeepers in Promise. He'd defrauded them, humiliated them, and ultimately *she* was the one to blame. Savannah didn't know if she could forgive herself. "I should've let Grady kick him out that first day," she muttered fiercely.

"You don't think he's coming back?"

She shook her head. "All his things are gone."

"Everything?"

She nodded and swallowed tightly. "Including Grady's truck."

Laredo swore under his breath. "Did Grady talk to Sheriff Hennessey?" he asked.

Savannah looked down at her clenched hands. "Yes," she said, her voice small. "That was when he learned…"

"Learned what?"

She sighed. "There's more, Laredo. Richard's charged thousands of dollars' worth of goods in Promise. He owes money to everyone in town. There was never any check. He didn't intend to pay for any of the things he charged and now he's gone." She squeezed her eyes shut in an effort to keep the tears at bay. "You should have seen the look on Grady's face when Frank told him. It was the same look he had six years ago—when he found out what Richard did then. After Mom and Dad died…"

Savannah hadn't thought herself capable of such intense anger. She looked her husband in the eye and said, "I think I hate my own brother."

Chapter Eight

Richard had been gone a week. To Grady, his brother's disappearance was both a blessing and a curse. Only now was Grady getting a complete picture of the damage Richard's extended visit had wrought. Every day since his brother had vanished, a fistful of new bills arrived, charges Richard had made using the family's accounts.

The bills were stacked on Grady's desk, and whenever he looked at them, his anger mounted. He'd made a list of money owed and checked it three or four times before he could grasp the full extent of what Richard had done.

While a majority of businesses in town accepted credit cards, ranchers tended to avoid them. Grady carried only one, and it was tucked in the back of his wallet for emergencies. All his purchases were paid for with cash or put on account, then paid in full at the end of each month.

In the weeks since his return, Richard had taken it upon himself to run into town to pick up supplies, and Grady had let him. Sending his worthless brother on errands had seemed innocent enough, and it freed up Laredo, Wiley and him for the more serious ranching chores. What Grady didn't know was that every time Richard had driven into town, he'd charged clothing, expensive liquor, all kinds of things, on the family accounts. It added up to nearly eight thousand dollars, not including the money still owed on some of his earlier purchases. Richard had masterfully hidden what he'd done, robbing Peter to pay Paul, returning goods and buying other things with the credits. He'd managed to disguise his actions using a number of clever cons. Merchants had trusted him. Trusted the Weston name.

Now Richard was gone, and just like six years earlier, Grady was stuck with the mess he'd left behind.

Unable to tolerate looking at the stack of past due notices, Grady grabbed his hat and abandoned his office. The day was hot, although it was only nine in the morning, and he was supposed to meet Wiley and the hired hands near Gully Creek.

He was halfway to the barn when he saw Frank Hennessey's patrol car coming down the driveway, kicking up a plume of dust in its wake. Grady paused and waited for the lawman. With any luck Frank would have some word about Richard and the stolen truck. Whereas Grady hadn't filed charges against his brother six years ago, he felt no such compulsion now. He wanted Richard found and prosecuted to the full extent of the law.

Richard deserved a jail term, if for nothing more than the agony he'd caused Caroline by kidnapping Maggie. Until the day he died, Grady wouldn't understand what had prompted his brother to steal away with the child.

For her part Maggie seemed to have made a full recovery. Thank God. She clung to Caroline, but that was understandable. She refused to talk about where she'd gone or who she'd been with, but anyone with half a brain knew it'd been Richard. If Grady had anything for which to thank his useless brother, it was that he'd had had the common decency to bring Maggie back to her mother.

Frank parked the patrol car in the yard and slowly climbed out of the driver's seat. "Morning, Grady." He touched the brim of his hat.

"Frank." Grady nodded in greeting. "I hope you've come with good news."

"Good and bad, I'm afraid," Frank said. By tacit agreement the two men headed toward the house for coffee. Savannah was busy in her office, updating her rose catalog on the computer, but she'd recently put on a fresh pot.

Grady poured them each a cup but didn't sit down. When it was a question of receiving news about Richard, he preferred to do it standing up.

"What have you learned?" Grady asked, after giving Frank a moment to taste the coffee. He leaned against the kitchen counter and crossed his ankles. Frank remained standing, as well.

"First, your truck's been found."

This was an unexpected and pleasant surprise. Grady had driven the old Ford pickup for ten years now, and he'd grown attached to it. The thought of being forced to buy a new one had rankled, especially in light of the mounting bills.

"Richard abandoned it in Brewster," Frank said, "and stole another."

While he wasn't surprised, Grady would almost rather lose his truck permanently than have his own brother steal some other rancher's vehicle.

"It was a newer model," Frank said with a soft snicker. "Apparently yours was a bit too old to suit his image."

Grady didn't miss the sheriff's well-placed sarcasm.

"Only this truck had an additional advantage," Frank muttered.

"What's that?"

"The owner kept a rifle mounted in the back window."

Grady took a moment to mull over the information. "You don't think Richard would actually use it, do you?"

The lawman shrugged. "Given the right set of circumstances, I wouldn't put it past him."

Grady had never thought of Richard as violent. He'd proved himself to be a weasel and a lowlife, but the fact that he might be brutal enough to use a weapon against another human being surprised even Grady. "What makes you think that?" Grady asked, afraid of what Frank was going to say. Last night he'd alluded briefly to something Richard had done back East, but at the time they were all too concerned about Maggie to give it much thought. "What do you know about Richard?"

The sheriff had never been one to hedge, and he didn't do so now. "It gives me no pleasure to tell you this, but there's been an arrest warrant issued for him from New York City."

"New York? On what charge?"

"The list is as long as my arm," Frank said with real regret. "Extortion for one. Richard's been involved in a number of scams, most of them bilking immigrants from Central and South America. Apparently he fed them a pack of lies, luring them into the country with promises of housing and jobs. Promises he had no intention of keeping. He set them up in warehouses in horrible conditions, forced them into menial jobs from which he collected most of their pay. It made big news on the East Coast when his activities were uncovered. Somehow he managed to scrape together the bail, then hit the road the minute he was freed."

Grady had been angry at his brother and furious at himself, too, for allowing Richard to worm his way back into their lives with his hard-luck story. Richard had taken advantage of his family; that was bad enough. But to learn he'd made a profession of stealing from others made Grady sick. How was it that his own brother—born of the same two parents, raised in the same household—could have lowered himself to such depths? If he lived to be an old man, Grady would never understand what had turned Richard into the type of person who purposely hurt others.

"I'm sorry to be the one to tell you this, Grady," Frank said again.

"I realize that." His voice sounded strange even to his own ears.

"When and if we find Richard, I won't have any choice but to arrest him."

"I understand." Grady wouldn't expect anything less. It was what his brother deserved.

"I talked to the New York district attorney this morning. The state wants him bad. Apparently there's been quite a bit of press regarding his arrest and the charges brought against him. He's hurt a lot of people, Grady."

"What happened to him? What made Richard the way he is?" The questions were rhetorical; Grady didn't actually expect the sheriff to supply an answer.

Frank shook his head. "Hell if I know. I liked Richard. He was always charming and clever—but somehow that turned into conniving and untrustworthy. Why he's like that, I couldn't say. Over the years I've met other people who were just as rotten, and I don't believe environment or bad circumstances is always the explanation. Your parents were God-fearing folk, and they raised him right. The fault lies within Richard himself."

Although Grady already knew as much, it helped to have a lawman as experienced as Frank confirm it.

"Eventually Richard will be caught," Frank said, as if he felt the necessity to prepare Grady for the inevitable. "And when he is, he'll be headed straight for prison."

It hurt to think of his brother doing jail time, but Grady's sympathies went out to all the people Richard had cheated, himself included.

Grady walked Frank out to his patrol car, then made his way to the barn. He whistled for Rocket and stopped abruptly when the dog didn't come. Rocket's hearing was getting bad, and he'd grown arthritic; these days, he mostly enjoyed lazing about on the front porch. But he still liked to accompany Grady to the barn. Just to reassure himself, Grady decided to check on his dog. Rocket had belonged to his father and was already middle-aged—seven years old—at the time of the accident. In the hard, financially crippling years that followed, the dog had become Grady's constant sidekick and friend. He'd shared his woes, frustrations, joys and sorrows with Rocket, and the old dog always gave him comfort.

A smile came to him when he saw the dog lying on his usual braided rug. He whistled again. "Come on, boy, we've got work to do."

Rocket remained still.

As Grady approached, the front porch, his steps slowed. He wasn't sure when he realized his faithful companion was gone, but by the time he reached the porch steps, his heart was full of dread.

"Rocket," he whispered, and hunkered down beside the dog.

One touch confirmed the worst. Rocket had died, apparently in his sleep.

An intense sadness settled over Grady. On a ranch dogs came and went, and he'd learned the downfall of becoming too attached to any one animal. But Rocket was special. Different. Rocket was a loyal, intelligent dog—the best dog he'd ever had; Rocket was also the last tangible piece of his father.

His throat ached and he bowed his head for several minutes, not even trying to fight back the tears.

Once he'd composed himself, he sought out his sister. He found her working in her garden. "I need a shovel," he announced without emotion, as if he didn't know where one was kept.

As he knew she would, Savannah guessed immediately that something wasn't right. "What happened?"

He steeled himself and told her. "Rocket's gone. It looks like he died in his sleep."

He watched as the sadness transformed her face. Tears filled her eyes. "Oh, Grady, I'm so sorry. I now how much you loved him."

"He was just a dog," he said with a stoicism he didn't feel.

"Not an ordinary dog," she added gently.

"No, not ordinary," he agreed, the pain of loss tightening his chest. "If you agree, I'd like to bury him in your garden by the rosebush you named after Mom."

She nodded mutely.

They worked side by side, brother and sister. Grady dug the grave, grateful for the physical effort that helped vent his pain. Again and again he was forced to remind himself that Rocket was just a dog, like a dozen or more who'd lived and died through the years. But he couldn't make himself believe it.

When he finished, he placed a rock as a marker. Savannah stood beside him.

"Goodbye, Rocket," she whispered.

"Goodbye, old friend," Grady said.

Savannah sobbed and turned into his arms. Grady held her, battling back emotion himself. An image came to mind, a memory—his father crouched down and Rocket running toward him, leaping into his arms, joyfully licking his face. Their reunion would be a happy one, but Grady knew there'd be a hole in his heart for a long time to come.

"IM GLAD we could finally meet for lunch," Ellie Frasier said, sliding into the booth at the bowling alley café.

Jane Dickinson smiled in welcome. She'd been waiting ten minutes, but she tended to be early, a habit her family had instilled in her. This lunch date was something she'd really looked forward to, although it had been difficult to arrange with both their schedules so busy. But Dovie had encouraged Jane to meet Ellie, mentioning her in almost every conversation.

Jane had come to think of Dovie as a mentor and friend. Stopping to talk with her that first morning she'd gone for a jog had been one of the smartest things she'd done since moving to Promise. Unfortunately Dovie was still the only person in town she knew on a first-name basis. Despite her efforts to become part of the community, friendly gestures from the other residents of Promise were few and far between.

"So…Dovie thought it would be a good idea for the two of us to get to know each other," Ellie said, reaching for the menu.

"I realize you're getting married soon," Jane said as a means of starting the conversation. "You must be terribly busy…."

Ellie nodded. "The wedding's only a couple of weeks away." A wistful look stole over her face.

Jane recognized that look—it was the look of a woman in love. Jane envied her happiness. After medical school and then working as an intern, followed by her residency at a huge public-health hospital in Los Angeles, there hadn't been time in her life for anything other than medicine. Now she was trapped in Texas with only one friend and zero prospects for romance.

Ellie did little more than glance at the menu before she set it aside.

Jane had spent several minutes reading over the selections, but had failed to make a choice. "You know what you're going to have?"

"I almost always order the chicken-fried steak."

The thought of all those fat grams was enough to make Jane feel queasy. Even the salads listed on the menu were ones she normally avoided—coleslaw with mayonnaise dressing, for instance. Most of the food was battered and fried. Even the vegetables. Okra coated in cornmeal and cooked in a deep fryer. The same with tomatoes. It was a wonder anyone lived beyond twenty-five in this town. The eating habits here were probably the unhealthiest she'd seen in years. It was time the people of Promise caught up with the latest information on health and diet.

"The chicken-fried steak is great," Ellie coaxed when Jane continued to study the menu.

The waitress arrived with her pad and pen. Ellie gave the woman her order, then chatted briefly while Jane reviewed her choices one last time.

"I'll have a green salad with avocado if you've got it."

The waitress—Denise, according to her name tag—wrote it down on her pad.

"With dressing on the side."

Denise exchanged a scornful glance with Ellie before she called the order in to the kitchen. The woman's reaction was typical of what Jane had encountered the past few weeks.

"What did I do that was so wrong?" Jane asked, leaning forward.

"First off, we Texans pride ourselves on our food."

"The diet around here is appalling," Jane blurted without thinking. "Everything is loaded with fat. Chicken-fried steak, barbecued meat, chili without beans—doesn't anyone appreciate the high fiber content of kidney beans?"

"It's exactly this attitude that's causing your problems, Doc."

"What attitude? All I'm trying to do is set better health standards for the community! It's a wonder you aren't all dead or dying."

"And a wonder you haven't been tarred and feathered," Ellie snapped.

Jane's mouth sagged open. She might have laughed if Ellie hadn't looked so serious.

"You want to know why people are unfriendly?" Ellie asked. "Perhaps you should look at how *you* come across. Rude, superior and know-it-all! The only reason I agreed to talk to you is because of Dovie, who for reasons I don't understand has taken a liking to you."

The woman was spitting mad, and other than pointing out a few basic truths, Jane still didn't know what she'd done that was so offensive.

"As far as everyone in this town is concerned, you can take your salad-eating wine-sipping butt and go back to California. We don't need some surfer chick telling us what's good for us, understand?"

Jane noted that the other customers had gone quiet. Several heads nodded in agreement. "I see," she said, struggling to hold on to her composure. "But unfortunately I've signed a contract and I'm stuck here for three years. So if I'm going to live in this community—"

"Then I suggest you change your high-and-mighty ways."

Swallowing her pride, Jane nodded. "I'm probably going to need a little help."

"You need a lot of help."

Jane decided to let that comment slide. "I'd appreciate a few words of advice."

Ellie didn't answer right away. "You sure you're up to this?"

Jane smiled. As far as she could see, she didn't have any choice. "Be gentle, all right?"

A smile cracked Ellie's lips. "I'll try."

Jane sighed. They'd started off on the wrong foot, but she sensed Ellie could be an important ally, and she badly needed a friend her own age. Dovie was kind, but it would take more than the assistance of one woman to help her fit in.

"Denise." Ellie waved her arm and called for the waitress. "Doc wants to change her order."

"I do?"

"You said you're willing to learn. Now's your chance. Your initiation, if you like. First, I'll teach you how to eat like a Texan. We can both diet tomorrow."

Jane swallowed, then nodded. "What is it I want to order?"

Ellie motioned to the waitress. "The doc here will have the chicken-fried steak, fried okra and an extra scoop of gravy on her mashed potatoes."

"All *right*," Denise said with smiling approval, writing it on her pad. "Do you want a side salad with that?" she asked.

It would probably be the only healthy part of the entire meal. "Sure." Jane was about to remind her to leave off the dressing, when Ellie added, "Put the dressing right on top of it, too, will you, Denise?"

The waitress grinned from ear to ear. "Not a problem."

Jane decided then and there that either she'd adjust to life in Texas...or die trying.

MAGGIE GASPED and bolted upright in bed, unsure for a moment where she was. Her skin felt clammy, and she was breathing fast. A moment later she realized it had only been a dream. She'd been in the town again, the one with the bad ghosts. Richard was in her dream, too. He was looking at her and his face kept getting wider and longer as if he were staring at her through a wavy mirror.

His voice boomed loud, too, and he kept telling her what would happen to her mother if Maggie told anyone where she'd been. Again and again she promised him she wouldn't tell, and she hadn't. Not anyone. Not even her dolls.

Kicking aside her blankets, Maggie stole out of the bedroom and sneaked down the hallway, guided by the nightlight, to her mother's bedroom. She stood and watched her mother sleeping, checking to make sure she was safe and no bad ghosts had gotten her.

"Maggie?" Her mother's eyes fluttered open.

"I had a bad dream," Maggie whispered.

Her mother tossed back the sheet, silently inviting Maggie into bed with her. Maggie was glad; it was a rare treat to sleep with her mommy. She climbed onto the bed and her mother wrapped an arm around her, then gently brushed the hair from her brow.

"Was it a very bad dream?" she asked.

"A scary one," Maggie told her.

"Do you want to tell me about it?"

Maggie shook her head. She didn't want to think about Richard ever again. She remembered that he didn't know she'd taken the doll, and if he found out, he might send the bad ghosts after her. As soon as she could, Maggie had removed the doll from her backpack and hidden it inside a big tin in her closet. No one knew it was there. Not Mommy. Not Richard. Not anyone.

Safe in her mother's arms, Maggie closed her eyes.

"You're not frightened now, are you?"

Maggie shook her head, but it wasn't true. "A little," she confessed.

"Did I tell you Grady's coming over tomorrow after church, and we're going to the park for a picnic?"

Maggie's spirits buoyed. "We are?" Usually they went out to the ranch and visited with Savannah and Laredo, too.

"Does that sound like fun?"

Maggie nodded eagerly. "Will Grady push me on the swing?"

"If you ask him."

Maggie closed her eyes again and sighed deeply. "Grady's not so bad. I'm sorry his dog died." She'd liked Rocket.

She felt her mommy nod. "He's going to miss him."

"I'm going to miss him, too," Maggie said. "Maybe we can make Grady feel better."

"He doesn't frighten you anymore?"

Maggie shook her head. "He does a little when he yells, but if I plug my ears I don't really hear it."

"He doesn't mean to yell, it's just…part of his nature."

Maggie wasn't entirely sure what that meant. But she knew that ever since the morning Grady found her running down the driveway and she saw his face light up with a smile, she'd liked him better. Until then, she'd never seen Grady smile, not a real smile, anyway. He'd hugged her again and again that day, and her mommy, too. Later he'd taken her into the barn and held her hand so she wouldn't be afraid of Widowmaker and let her see the new colt.

Grady had reminded her that she had yet to choose a name for him. She'd chosen "Moonbeam," and Grady said it was a pretty name. Wiley had teased him about it and said it sounded like one of those hippie names from the sixties—whatever that meant—but Grady had insisted Moonbeam was it. She'd chosen well.

"I think Grady's special," Maggie announced suddenly. She no longer felt any doubt. Richard had been fun at first, but he wasn't a real friend.

"I do, too," her mommy said softly.

CAROLINE HAD READIED the picnic basket and cooler before church, packing everything that didn't need to be refrigerated. It had been Grady's idea to go on a picnic in Pioneer Park and she suspected she knew why. Ever since she'd brought up the subject of Maggie's father, he'd been waiting for her to tell him. She wished now that she'd ignored his advice the day they'd gone horseback riding. The day Maggie disappeared. It would make everything far less complicated now. She pushed the worry to the back of her mind, determined to have a good time. If the subject arose, she'd deal with it then.

The park sat in the very center of town and took up four square blocks. It had a wading pool for toddlers, as well as Promise's one and only swimming pool, complete with diving board. The grass was lush and green and meticulously groomed. A statue of a pioneer family stood proudly in the middle, along with a plaque that described the pioneers' role in Texan history. The paved walkways all led directly toward the statue.

Maggie loved the playground, and Caroline appreciated Grady's willingness to indulge her child. Ever since that terrible night, Grady had given special attention to her daughter.

Caroline didn't know what she would have done without Grady. That night had been a turning point for all of them. For her and Grady, and for Grady and Maggie.

The doorbell rang and Maggie screamed from inside her bedroom, ''I'll get it!'' Caroline heard her race for the door.

The only person it could be was Grady. He'd followed them home from church, driving the old Ford pickup, which had been returned to him a few days before. Maggie had already changed out of her Sunday-school dress and into shorts. Caroline wore a sleeveless yellow cotton dress, with a wide straw hat and sandals, the same clothes she'd worn to the service. Grady sent her a purely masculine look of approval as Maggie dragged him by the hand into the kitchen.

''It's Grady,'' Maggie announced unnecessarily. ''Can we go now?''

"Soon. I've got to load up the potato salad and fried chicken first."

"Mommy makes the best potato salad in the world," Maggie said. "She lets me peel the hard-boiled eggs and help her stir."

"No wonder it's so good," he said, and glanced from Maggie to Caroline.

The look, however brief, made Caroline wonder if he was speculating about who had fathered her child. Then again, she might be imagining it. Every time they were together, she became obsessed with her secret, with the need to tell Grady. She loved this man and she feared what would happen once he learned the truth.

"Go put on your running shoes," Caroline instructed her daughter. Maggie dashed out of the room, eager to comply.

Grady watched Maggie go before turning his attention to her. "I didn't embarrass you in church this morning, did I?"

"No," she answered, wondering what he was talking about.

"I couldn't keep my eyes off you."

"I didn't really notice…" She hated this tension, this constant fear that any look he gave her, any silence, meant he was wondering about Maggie's father. Soon, she promised herself. She'd tell him soon. Perhaps even today.

Grady gripped her about the waist and they kissed, sweetly and unhurriedly. "I didn't hear a word of Wade's sermon," he whispered into her hair, holding her close.

"Me, neither." But not for the reasons he assumed.

"Wade stopped me on the way out the door," Grady said, grinning, "and told me there'd be a test on the sermon next week. Not to worry, though, he was willing to share his notes."

Caroline managed a smile. "I think Wade's the best thing that's happened to Promise Christian in a long time."

"You're the best thing that's happened to me," Grady whispered. "Ever." He reluctantly let her go when Maggie tore into the kitchen.

The five-year-old was breathless with excitement. "I'm ready!" she cried.

Caroline added the potato salad and fried chicken to the cooler, and Grady carried it to his pickup. The three of them piled into the front and drove to the park.

Caroline noticed that Maggie was especially quiet on the short drive. She was concerned the child might be reacting to her tension. But Maggie's spirits lifted the instant they arrived at the park. Grady lugged the picnic supplies to a vacant table, and while Caroline covered it with a plastic-coated tablecloth, Maggie insisted on showing Grady her favorite swing.

"Go on, you two," Caroline said, waving them away. Once again she noticed—or thought she did—the way Grady studied Maggie. Briefly she wondered if he'd guessed.

Determined to ignore her worries, at least for the moment, Caroline spread a blanket on the grass in a shady area. When she'd finished, she slid the cooler beneath the table and out of the sun.

The sound of Maggie's laughter drifted toward her, and Caroline looked up to discover her daughter on the swing set with Grady standing behind her.

"Higher!" Maggie shouted. "Push me higher!"

Grady did, until Caroline held her breath at the heights the swing reached. She pressed her hand to her mouth to keep from calling out a warning, knowing she could trust Grady with her daughter. She gasped once when the swing buckled, but Grady swiftly caught it and brought it back under control.

Eventually he stopped the swing and Maggie returned to

earth. Squealing with delight, she still had energy left to run back to their picnic table.

"Did you see, Mommy?" Maggie cried. "Did you see how high Grady pushed me?"

Caroline nodded. "I saw."

"I could touch the sky with my feet. Did you see? Did you see?"

"Yes, baby, I saw."

The afternoon was lovely. After they ate, Maggie curled up on the blanket and quickly fell asleep.

Now, Caroline commanded herself. *Tell him now.* But she couldn't make herself do it, couldn't bear to see the look in his eyes when he learned the truth. Avoiding his gaze, she brushed the soft curls from her daughter's brow.

"Any effects from her night away from home?" Grady asked. "Has she told you anything of what happened?"

"Not a word, but she woke up last night with a nightmare and wouldn't tell me about it."

"Poor thing."

Caroline gazed down at her slumbering child, loving her with an intensity that went beyond anything she'd ever known, even the strong love she felt for Grady. "She's back, safe and sound, and for that I'm grateful."

"I am, too."

Caroline leaned against Grady, letting him support her weight, his hands resting on her shoulders.

"Savannah reminded me that it's Maggie's birthday next week. I'd like to give her something special, but I need to ask you about it first. She seems quite taken with Moonbeam, so—"

"You're giving her the colt?" Caroline could barely believe her ears. At the same time she realized that the mention of Maggie's birthday created a natural opening to talk about her child's father. To reveal his name.

No! she couldn't tell him, Caroline thought in sudden panic.

"Of course we'll keep Moonbeam at the ranch."

While the offer was tempting, horses weren't cheap to maintain.

"The gift includes room and board." Grady answered her question even before she could ask it.

"That's generous of you."

"She's going to be six, right?"

"Yes."

His gaze softened as he studied the little girl. "You said once that you'd dated Cal."

Caroline felt as though her lungs had frozen. This was as close as Grady had come to asking her outright about Maggie's father.

"I did," she said, and looked away. He reached for her hand. "Now that Richard's gone—"

"Do you mind if we don't talk about my brother?" Grady said, interrupting her. "I want to escape him for a few hours if I can."

"Of course, but—"

"I'd much rather concentrate on other things just now, like how good you feel in my arms."

Caroline closed her eyes.

"It doesn't matter, Caroline," he whispered close to her ear.

"What doesn't matter?"

"About Maggie. I already love her."

"I know. It's just that…" Caroline liked to think she would have continued if Maggie hadn't chosen that precise moment to awake.

"Can we go swing again?" she asked Grady.

He grinned. "This time let's bring your mother, too. All right?"

Maggie took Caroline's hand and the three of them

headed toward the swing set, the subject she was about to broach shelved once again.

The day ended far sooner than Caroline and Maggie would have wished. Grady dropped them off at seven and went to check in with Frank Hennessey. Caroline assumed it had to do with Richard, but she didn't ask and he didn't volunteer.

The light on her answering machine was flashing, and while she unpacked the picnic basket, she played it back.

"It's Savannah. Give me a call when you get home."

Tucking the phone to her ear, Caroline punched out her friend's number. As she waited for Savannah to answer, she set the leftovers in the refrigerator.

"Hi, it's me, Caroline. You called?" she asked when Savannah picked up the receiver.

"I did." Savannah sounded pleased about something, but didn't elaborate. In fact, she appeared to be waiting for Caroline to speak first.

"Um, Savannah, was there a particular reason you called?" Caroline finally ventured.

"Aren't you going to tell me, or is it a big secret?"

"Savannah, *what* are you talking about?"

The line went silent. "He didn't ask you?"

"Ask me what?"

"Oh, dear," Savannah said with an exaggerated sigh. "When he left this morning, Grady was as fidgety as a drop of cold water on a hot skillet."

"Maybe he's got heat rash," Caroline teased. "Now tell me what this is all about."

"Grady," Savannah said, as if that much should be obvious. "And then in church, the poor man couldn't keep his eyes off you."

"This isn't making a lot of sense, Savannah Smith."

"And I was so sure, too."

"Sure about what?" Caroline demanded.

"That Grady was going to ask you to marry him."

Chapter Nine

Every pew in Promise Christian Church was filled for the wedding of Ellie Frasier and Glen Patterson. Glen had asked Cal to be his best man and Grady to serve as one of the ushers. Grady had agreed before he learned that he was expected to wear a tuxedo. He wasn't sure how a man could breathe with a shirt buttoned up that tight.

The main advantage of being in the wedding party was that Caroline was one of Ellie's bridesmaids. Grady had never realized that four women all wearing the same dresses could look so different. In his—admittedly biased—opinion, Caroline was the most beautiful. Savannah, of course, was a close second.

Since it was the hottest time of the year, Wade McMillen kept his sermon short. Ellie and Glen exchanged their vows as both their mothers sat in the front row quietly weeping. The Moorhouse sisters sobbed loudly, and Dovie Boyd dabbed at her eyes, as well. Even the coolly composed Dr. Dickinson, sitting beside Dovie, sniffled a bit as the *I do*'s were said.

Grady met Frank Hennessey's eye as they exited the church. Frank had his arm protectively around Dovie, and his expression seemed to say that he had plenty of years on Grady and he still didn't understand what made women weep at weddings.

The reception was held at the Grange hall and, on this Saturday afternoon, there were as many cars parked out front as the night of the big summer dance. The table closest to the door was stacked high with elegantly wrapped wedding gifts.

Grady ended up spending most of his time in the reception line, but once again he was compensated by having Caroline at his side.

"Ellie looks so beautiful," she said when the last guest had made her way through the line.

Grady's patience when it came to these formal affairs was limited. He felt tired and hungry. "Do you want something to eat?" he asked with a longing glance at the buffet table.

"I've got to help Ellie change out of her wedding dress," she told him.

"You mean we can take off these fancy duds?" He eased his index finger between the starched collar and his neck.

"Not us. Just Ellie and Glen."

"Not fair," he complained.

"Go help yourself to some dinner and I'll be back before you know it." She kissed his cheek, and while it was only a sample of what he wanted, he'd take what he could get.

"Where'd Caroline go?" Cal asked, coming up behind Grady in the buffet line.

"To help Ellie change out of her dress." Grady thought that made him sound like an expert on wedding etiquette, but he wouldn't have had a clue if Caroline hadn't told him.

"Who designed these starched shirts, anyway?" Cal muttered, "The Marquis de Sade?"

"I wouldn't doubt it." Grady reached for a plate. It'd been hours since he'd last eaten. Between that and the afternoon's exertions, he was starved.

"Glen's a married man now," Cal said as if it had only now hit him.

"Does that bother you?" Grady asked, thinking there'd be a big adjustment in Cal's life. Grady had heard, Glen was moving into town with Ellie; apparently, they'd put money down on a house.

"Doesn't bother me at all—but it would if he hadn't married Ellie. Those two are good together."

Grady felt the same way. Cal and Glen had been his neighbors all his life. Neighbors and best friends. The three of them were as close as family, and yet Grady had to wonder if he knew Cal as well as he thought he did. Again and again he'd mulled over the news that Cal had once dated Caroline, but he firmly believed Cal would have married her if he'd been the baby's father.

Grady had given up trying to work out who Maggie's father was. He felt certain it had to be someone he knew, perhaps trusted, otherwise she wouldn't hesitate to tell him. Whenever they were together he watched her struggle with herself. The one time she'd been ready to tell him, he'd stopped her. He wanted to kick himself for that now. This secret was tormenting her—and him, too.

Last Sunday on their picnic, he'd tried to reassure her that it didn't matter. He loved Maggie and he loved her. Apparently he'd failed, because she seemed more apprehensive than ever.

"Glen looks at Ellie the way you look at Caroline," Cal said casually.

"It's that noticeable, is it?"

Cal nodded. "You could say that."

They carried their plates to a recently vacated table in the far corner of the hall.

Grady stacked the empty plates to one side and pulled out a chair. Cal sat across from him. "I'm thinking of asking Caroline to marry me," he said, mentioning it in an offhand way. It was the first time he'd said it aloud. He watched Cal's reaction, closely.

"All right!" Cal grinned. "I wondered how long it'd take you. I've always liked Caroline."

"I love her." Grady had no problem admitting it, and if Cal had any leftover emotion for her, he'd rather they cleared the air now.

"Then what's the holdup?"

Grady felt a surge of anger, not at the question but at the answer. He stabbed his fork into a thick slice of ham as he waited for the bitterness to leave him. This was a day of shared joy, and he refused to allow his brother to ruin it.

Cal propped his elbows on the table. "My guess would be that Richard's got something to do with this. I thought he wasn't around anymore."

Without elaborating, Grady told him about the latest fiasco involving Richard. Cal and Frank Hennessey were the only two people with whom Grady would discuss his worthless brother. He supposed Cal had told Glen; that was only natural, and fine with him. Six years earlier, when Richard had disappeared with the inheritance money, Cal had advised Grady to press charges against him. Grady had agonized over it and in the end decided not to. Now he wondered if he'd made the right decision.

Few other people knew of Richard's treachery.

Savannah might have told Caroline, but he couldn't be sure. Of all the women in town, Caroline had been the most sensible about Richard and his attentions. Grady admired her for seeing through his brother and not being taken in by his easy charm. Nearly everyone had been deceived by his flattery and suave ways, but not her.

"Richard's gone," Grady said, answering his friend, "and yet he isn't. He left behind damn near eight thousand dollars in debts."

Cal gave a low whistle.

Grady told him how his brother had charged things on local accounts all around town. Clothes, liquor, food, even camping and ranch supplies, although God only knew what he intended to do with them. Frankly, Grady didn't *want* to know.

"They aren't your debts," Cal was quick to remind him. "The bills have Richard's signature on them."

"But he put them on the family accounts."

Cal sighed in resignation. "You paid them, didn't you?"

"I didn't have any choice." It was the Weston name that stood to be tarnished. Grady knew he wouldn't be able to look his friends and neighbors in the eye when his own brother had bilked them, unless he himself made good on the debts. Which he had. That eight thousand had nearly wiped out his savings, but he'd get by, just as he always had.

Earlier in the week he'd checked out engagement rings in the jeweler's window, and he'd realized he wouldn't be able to buy as big a diamond as he wanted for Caroline; he also realized it was more important to be debt-free.

Cal was about to ask him something else when Frank Hennessey abruptly pulled out a chair and joined them. He cast them a grateful look. "I'm safe for now," he said in a low voice.

"Safe from who?" Grady asked, puzzled. Frank normally didn't run from anything or anyone.

Frank threw back his head with a groan. "Dovie. The woman's got that look in her eye again."

Cal and Grady exchanged glances. "What look?" Cal ventured.

"Marriage. I...I've been telling her for the last ten years that one day I'd marry her. I meant it at the time, but I tell you, boys, the mere thought is enough to make my blood run cold. I can see now I'm not the marrying kind—I'm just not! I've got to get *her* to see that." He hunched forward. "But I don't want to upset her, either."

"I thought—assumed that you and Dovie had, you know, an understanding," Grady whispered.

"We do," Frank said. "But every once in a while she reminds me of that stupid promise and I find an excuse to delay it, and she's satisfied for another few months. Then we attend a wedding or one of her friends has an anniversary, and she brings the subject up again. You'd think after this length of time, she'd figure we've got a pretty good arrangement. You'd think she'd be willing to leave well enough alone." He gave a long-suffering sigh. "I'm crazy about Dovie, but marriage isn't for me."

Grady began to speak, but Frank cut him off. "Weddings are dangerous things, boys. Dovie took one whiff of those orange blossoms, and next thing I knew she had that look."

"Why does she want to get married?" Cal asked, voicing Grady's own thoughts. If she'd been content for ten years without a ring on her finger, she obviously wasn't as keen on marriage as she let on.

"Dovie says a ten-year courtship is long enough. Either I follow through or this is it." Frank shook his head sadly. "I should never have said anything to her about marriage," he muttered, "but I couldn't help myself. I thought I'd lose her if I didn't propose, so I…sort of…did. At the time I actually believed we could make a go of it. Now I know marriage just wouldn't work. Not for me, anyway."

"Give her time to accept reality," Grady suggested.

Frank shook his head in despair. "You don't know Dovie like I do."

"You're sure you don't want to marry her?" The question came from Cal. Cal's mother and Dovie were good friends.

"It isn't that at all," Frank said. "I don't want to get

married, period. It has nothing to do with Dovie. She's the best thing that ever happened to me.''

''But you told her you would.''

''I know,'' Frank admitted. ''The thing is, most of the time she's as happy with our arrangement as I am. We live separate lives. She has her shop and her interests, and I have mine, and we both like it that way. We see each other just about every day, and hell, she knows how I feel about her.''

''But you won't marry her, no matter what?''

''I told you, marriage and I aren't compatible.'' Frank looked at them mournfully. ''I like my life just the way it is.'' The sheriff slowly exhaled. ''The two of you understand, don't you, seeing that neither one of you is married, either?''

Cal glanced quickly at Grady, eyebrows raised. ''This isn't a good time to be asking Grady that,'' he said.

''What?'' Frank said with a moan. ''You aren't thinking about getting married, are you?''

''As a matter of fact, I am.''

Frank swore under his breath. ''Caroline, isn't it?''

Grady nodded, not hiding his grin.

''She's a fine woman, but damn it all, this is going to send Dovie into wedding overdrive.''

''I haven't asked Caroline yet,'' Grady said.

''Thank God, because once Dovie learns you two got engaged, I won't hear the end of it.''

''I can't guarantee Caroline's answer.''

''Do you honestly think she'll refuse?'' Frank asked in a way that said he knew the answer. ''It's fairly obvious how you feel about each other.''

''Naturally I'm hoping....''

''Why borrow trouble?'' Cal asked. ''Of course she'll say yes. Why shouldn't she?''

TEN YEARS, Dovie mused darkly. She'd wasted ten years of her life on that ungrateful lawman. Arms folded, she paced her living room, back and forth, back and forth, trying to walk off her anger.

It wasn't working.

By the time they left Ellie and Glen's wedding reception, Dovie was barely speaking to Frank. He didn't have a lot to say, either—which was just as well. He'd proposed to her shortly after they'd met, and all these years she'd waited. All these years she'd believed in him and hoped and loved him.

Well, she'd better smarten up and accept the truth. Frank never intended to marry her, and really, why should he? He enjoyed all the delights of married life with none of the responsibilities. Twice a week he spent the night, and in the morning she made him breakfast and handed him his clean laundry and sent him on his way with a kiss.

No more.

There'd been only one other man in Dovie's life, and that was her husband. But Marvin had been dead thirteen years now. And for ten of those years she'd pined after a lawman who claimed to love her, but apparently not enough to marry her.

A light knock sounded on her back door. It had to be Frank Hennessey—the only person in the entire world who came to her in the dark of night. And Dovie knew why he'd come. Well, he could forget it. She had a thing or two to say to him.

She marched through the house and threw open the door, startling Frank.

"If you're here for the reason I think you are, then you can turn around and go right back home." She pointed in the direction of his parked car.

He blinked. "Dovie, sweetheart, you don't mean that."

He removed his hat and wore the anguished look of a mis-understood and badly maligned male.

"I certainly do mean it, Franklin Hennessey." She would have slammed the door on him, but he'd stuck his foot in.

"We have a good life just the way it is," he said enticingly.

"If I'm so happy about our lives, then why do I feel this ache in my heart? Why can't I sit through a wedding without dissolving in tears? I want you to marry me, Frank."

The pained expression returned. "Oh, Dovie, I can't do that."

"Can't or won't, Frank?"

He didn't answer and she knew why.

"I love you, Dovie." The words were a low purr.

"You *say* you love me, but you won't do anything to prove it," she spit, folding her arms and refusing to look at him.

"I can't tell you how sorry I am. I always thought…I believed one day I'd be able to…to take the plunge. But I realize now that marriage would never work for someone like me."

"Then we're at an impasse. I guess the reality is that you won't marry me. Not now and not ever."

"But it's not because I don't love you!"

"So either I accept you the way you are or—"

"Our arrangement has worked so far, hasn't it, my love?" he asked his eyes pleading.

"Or I break off this dead-end relationship," she continued, ignoring his words.

Frank went pale. "Oh, Dovie, you wouldn't do that."

Dovie drew a deep breath and the anger vanished. A peace of sorts came over her, a calmness. "I have to, Frank—for my own self-respect, if nothing else."

He stared at her as though he didn't understand.

It hurt to say the words, but either she did this or she'd never be able to face herself in the mirror again. Squaring her shoulders, she smiled sadly and said, "It'd be best if we didn't see each other anymore."

The sheriff's mouth dropped open. "Dovie, please! Be reasonable about this."

"It's over, Frank." She straightened and looked him straight in the eye.

"Okay," he agreed, unmistakable regret in his voice. "If that's the way you want it."

Dovie's hand gripped the door handle. "Goodbye, Frank," she said.

"Good night, Dovie." As though in a daze, he turned and left.

Tears clouded her eyes, but she refused to let them fall. She'd loved Frank for ten years, and it would be a major adjustment to untangle her life from his, but she'd do it and be a stronger woman for it.

A loud knock on the windowpane of her back door made her jump. Dovie answered it to find a bewildered-looking Frank standing on the other side.

"I just want to be sure we understand each other," he said, holding his hat in both hands. "Are you saying you don't want me stopping by on Wednesday and Saturday nights anymore?"

She rolled her eyes. "That's exactly what I'm saying."

"I see." He seemed to ponder her words for a moment. "What about dinners on Sunday?"

"I think we should put an end to that, as well."

"Afternoon tea at your shop?"

"You can find some other woman to spend your afternoon break with," she suggested, even though the thought of him seeing anyone else nearly destroyed her.

"There isn't another woman in the world I'd rather be with than you."

A slow smile eased up the corners of her mouth. "Then the answer is simple. Marry me the way you promised."

Frank ground his teeth. "I can't, Dovie. I wish to hell I could, but it's impossible. I just can't do it."

"There are certain things I can't do, either, Frank." She softly closed the door.

CAROLINE KNEW this dinner was different the minute Grady phoned to invite her. He was formal and polite—as if he was planning something other than a casual evening out.

"He's going to ask you," Savannah insisted. "I'm sure of it." It'd been a week since Ellie and Glen's wedding, and the topic of love and marriage hadn't strayed far from her best friend's mind.

"Have you thought about how you'll respond when he does?"

Caroline had thought of little else for an entire week. Not her response, should he bring up the question of marriage, but *his* response once she told him the truth about Maggie. The conversation lay before her like a stretch of deep, treacherous water. They'd need to get through that before she'd be able to consider her reply.

She figured he'd introduce the matter of marriage over dinner. Everything pointed to that. Rumor had it that he'd been seen in the jewelry store earlier in the week. In fact, he'd made a number of trips into town.

He'd stopped by the post office three times, which was highly unusual. If she saw him in town even once a week that was a surprise; three times was almost unheard of.

Maggie was spending the night at Dovie's, so Caroline had the luxury of a free afternoon in which to indulge herself without the constant interruptions of a six-year-old. She soaked in a perfume-scented tub, painted her toenails and curled her hair with a hot iron, all the while praying everything would go smoothly.

This was supposed to be the night of her dreams. But by the time Grady arrived to pick her up, she was a nervous wreck. The hours of anticipating his reaction had left her tense and jittery. Not knowing how he'd feel, what he'd say, was almost more than she could take.

The doorbell rang precisely at six, reminding her that even in small things, Grady Weston was reliable, a man who kept his word. His eyes widened with appreciation when he saw her, and she realized every minute she'd spent in front of the mirror had been worth it.

"I didn't think it was possible for you to look more beautiful than you did at Ellie's wedding," he said with the sincerity of a man not accustomed to giving compliments.

"Thank you." She twirled around to give him a full view of her new dress. "Do you like it?"

"Oh-h-h, yes."

"Where's Maggie?" he asked, glancing around.

"With Dovie. She's spending the night."

He handed her a bottle of wine, as if he'd suddenly remembered it was in his hands.

"Shall I open it now?" she asked.

"Sure. If you want."

He followed her into the kitchen, and as she searched for a corkscrew, she saw him pacing the room, his lips moving.

"Grady?"

His head shot up and he looked startled.

"Did you say something?"

He shook his head in quick denial.

She found the corkscrew and gave it to him. While he wrestled with the cork, Caroline took out two wineglasses.

"This isn't going to work," he announced, and set the bottle down on the countertop, the cork half-out.

"That's the only corkscrew I have," she said.

"I'm not talking about the wine." He pulled out a kitchen chair and with both hands on her shoulders urged her to sit. Then he finished opening the wine, a white zinfandel, and poured them each a glass.

He drank down the first one in three gulps; after that, he immediately refilled his glass.

"If your parents were alive, I'd talk to them…but it's just you and me. So—I'll say what I have to say."

"What you have to say?" she repeated, her eyebrows arched. Despite her own anxiety, she couldn't help enjoying his discomfort. Just a little.

He pointed his finger at her as he struggled with the words. "I have to do this now. If I wait any longer, I'll say or do something stupid, and the entire evening will be ruined." His eyes were warm, openly revealing his love. "And that isn't what I want."

"What *do* you want, Grady?" she asked, in a soft voice.

He reached for his wine and took a deep swallow.

"Wine is usually sipped," she murmured.

"I know," he said, "but I need the fortification."

Caroline's heart swelled with emotion. "Oh, Grady, I love you so much."

He stared at her for a long wonder-filled moment. "I love you, too." He smiled then, sweetly. "I practiced this proposal a dozen times on the drive into town, and now I find myself completely at a loss. I don't know where the hell to start."

"The fact that you love me is a good opening."

"But I have to tell you so much more."

"Love is only the beginning…" This was where she needed to explain the past, but she couldn't. Not now, in the most wonderfully romantic moment of her life. Not when the man she loved with all her heart was about to ask her to share his life.

"I'm free to love you," he said.

"Free?" she repeated, not understanding.

"Richard's gone."

She frowned and felt a sudden chill race down her bare arms. "What does Richard have to do with this?"

"Everything." She could feel the anger coming from him. She swallowed, waiting for him to elaborate.

"Richard has been a thorn in my side for six long years. He's my brother, and for that reason alone, a part of me will always love him. But I refuse to allow him to dictate my life a minute longer than he already has."

"What…what do you mean?"

"I'm finished dealing with the problems my brother created. I refuse to pick up any more of the pieces, or accept any further responsibility for the disasters he's left in his wake. I'm not paying another debt of his. Every minute of the last six years has been spent struggling to regain ground Richard stole from me. I resent every one of those wasted minutes, and I refuse to deal with his mistakes anymore."

Caroline wasn't sure how she could remain upright in her chair, why she didn't pitch to the ground.

The harshness left Grady's eyes as he looked at her. "As I said, I'm no longer tied to Richard or his troubles, so I can tell you how much I love you. Maggie, too." The anger dissipated and his features softened with love. "I'm free to ask you to share my life, Caroline, if you'll have me."

He hesitated, and when she didn't immediately respond, he said gently, "I'm asking you to marry me."

The choking in her throat made it impossible to respond.

"Is the decision that difficult?" He sounded a little hurt.

"No…"

"I did it all wrong, didn't I?" he muttered. He thrust a hand into his coat pocket and produced a velvet ring case. "Give me another chance to do this the way you deserve."

"Grady—"

"No, don't say anything. Not yet." Then he opened the small velvet box. "It took me thirty-six years to find the woman I want to be with for the rest of my life, and that woman is you, Caroline Daniels."

She pressed both hands over her mouth, her eyes filled with tears.

"Would you do me the honor of becoming my wife?"

She tried to speak and found that she couldn't.

"Just nod," he suggested.

"I can't," she finally managed, her voice cracking.

"Can't nod?"

"I can't marry you…" She stood up, then walked to the sink and stared out the window. This was the most difficult thing she'd ever done, outside of burying her mother. Only now she felt as if it was her heart she was laying to rest. Her heart. And her future.

"You're saying no?" He was clearly shocked.

"I can't because…" She stopped, unable to continue.

"You *can't* marry me?"

"No."

"Is that your final answer?"

She dared not turn around and look at him. "That's my final answer," she said in a monotone.

She heard him retreat, his heavy steps taking him as far as the living room. Without warning, he rushed back into the kitchen.

"Just one damn minute," he shouted. "I don't accept that. You just finished telling me how much you love me!"

She couldn't deny it and so she said nothing.

"If you're going to reject my proposal, then at least have the decency to look me in the eye when you do it."

Slowly, her heart breaking, she turned toward him.

"Tell me to my face that you don't want to marry me," he demanded.

Her chin came up. "I won't marry you."

Grady's jaw was clenched. *"Why not?"* The two words were like knives.

"Because if you married me..." she began, gazing straight ahead. She couldn't go on.

"I'm not good enough for you, is that it?"

"No!" This was said with all the conviction of her soul.

"Then say it," he yelled. "Just say it."

"Because if you married me," she started again, "you'd be left to deal with yet another one of Richard's mistakes."

He frowned darkly. Then he understood, and a look of horrified disbelief came over him. "Are you saying that *Richard* is Maggie's father?"

Caroline hung her head and nodded.

Chapter Ten

Richard was Maggie's father. Nothing Caroline could have told him would have shocked Grady more. The news went through him like a bolt of lightning. He was speechless with surprise, then numb with disbelief. Richard? His no-good cheating irresponsible brother was the father of Caroline's child? It was more than he could take in. More than he could accept.

Once his mind had cleared enough to let him respond, he asked the obvious questions. "When were you lovers? I don't remember the two of you so much as dating."

"We didn't, not in the normal sense." She reached for her wine. "I was in San Antonio in college, my senior year," she said, her voice low. "It was finals week. Knowing how crucial it was for me to do well, my mother didn't tell me what'd happened to your parents until after the exams. I felt horrible, sick to my stomach the moment she told me. I was furious with her for not letting me know. I'd always loved your mother. Your father, too." She inhaled deeply.

"You weren't at the funeral, were you?"

"No—because I didn't hear about it in time."

"Then how does Richard play into this?" He realized he sounded irritated; he couldn't help it. Damn it all, he was furious. Exasperated, too. The numbness was wearing off, and in its stead, a slow-burning anger began to build. Once again his brother had found a way to cheat him. Nothing in his life, *nothing,* was untainted by that bastard and his fiascos.

"San Antonio was his first stop after he took the money," Caroline continued.

Grady's eyes narrowed. "So you know about that? The theft?"

She nodded. "Savannah told me," she said. "Years later."

Grady pulled out a chair and sat down. He didn't think his knees would support him much longer.

"It was one of those flukes," Caroline went on. "I was gassing up at a service station and Richard pulled in. He didn't recognize me at first, but I told him how sorry I was about his parents." She looked away and took another steadying breath. "He seemed broken up about it."

"Broken up enough to walk away with the forty thousand dollars that was our inheritance," Grady mumbled.

"We had coffee together and he told me how he'd found your mother's and father's bodies."

"That's a lie!" Grady cried, knotting his fists in outrage. "Frank Hennessey found them and came and told us." How like Richard to seek all the sympathy!

"I know it's a lie now," she whispered, "but at the time I didn't have any reason not to believe him."

Grady vowed to stay quiet, seeing as every time he spoke, it interrupted the story, and this was one he very much wanted to hear.

"He broke into sobs and…and said he hadn't been able to bear the pain and after the funeral had blindly driven off, not knowing where he was going or how he'd gotten to San Antonio. He said he hadn't eaten or slept in days."

"And you believed him?" Grady shouted.

"He'd suffered a terrible loss." She raised her voice. "So, yes, I believed him."

Grady wiped a hand down his face. "I'm sorry, I didn't mean to yell."

"I...I didn't, either."

Despite the apology, he struggled with his temper. "It's something of a shock to learn that the woman I love has slept with my brother."

She didn't respond, but Grady could see that his words had hit their mark. He didn't want to hurt her, but he felt a sick ache in every part of his being, and lashing out was a natural response. Even when he knew he was being cruel and unfair. He hated himself for it, but couldn't seem to hold back.

To Caroline's credit she didn't retaliate or ask him to leave. He admired her restraint and wished his own response had been more generous, more forgiving. In time, perhaps, he could be, but not now. Definitely not now.

After a silence Caroline picked up her story. "He was an emotional mess and I took him home with me. We weren't in the house five minutes when he fell asleep on the sofa. I phoned my home and my mother confirmed that Richard had disappeared the afternoon of the funeral. I...I didn't tell her he was with me. I should have. I realized that too late, but my sympathies were with Richard. He'd received a terrible shock and—"

"No less terrible than what Savannah and I suffered."

"I know, but he was with me and you were here in Promise." She clenched her hands in her lap. "Don't you think I've gone over this a million times since? Don't you think I have my regrets, too?"

He nodded, hating himself for being angry and unable to keep his emotions under control. Every time he thought about Richard being Maggie's father, a fierce kind of outrage gripped him.

"Do…do you want me to continue?"

"Yes," he replied, mentally preparing himself for what was to follow.

"According to Richard, he was overcome with grief, running from his pain and…and he'd found me."

"It was fate, right?" Grady's sarcasm was heavy.

"Yes…"

"He spent the night?"

"Yes." Her voice grew small. "I made up a bed in the living room for him, but in the middle of the night he came into my bedroom and said he needed someone to hold."

"And you let him?"

"Yes."

"I suppose he felt all better in the morning, then?"

"Grady, it wasn't like that."

Her voice grew strong, then defiant. He stared at her, and for a moment almost hated her. But it wasn't possible; he loved her too much. No one else possessed the power to hurt him like this. Loving Caroline and Maggie had brought him such joy, but it made him vulnerable, too. Vulnerable to pain and to anger. Vulnerable to a lot of emotions that were unfamiliar to him. Uncomfortable emotions.

He wasn't sure he wanted to experience them again, not if it made him feel like this.

All at once sitting became intolerable and he jumped to his feet. "Was it rape?"

She took a long time answering. "No. That's not Richard's way. But I was inexperienced and he…he used my naïveté."

It came to Grady, then, what she was telling him. "He seduced you, didn't he?"

"I was young and a virgin. I thought he was the most handsome man in the world. He was hurting—both his parents had died in a tragic accident—and he'd turned to me for comfort. I didn't mean to let him make love to me, but he was so convincing, and before I realized what was happening, he was in bed with me, kissing me, telling me how much he needed me to take away this terrible pain. I tried to tell him I couldn't do that, but he wouldn't listen and then…he climbed on top of me and—"

"How long did he stay at your place?" Grady asked, thinking how desperately he and Savannah had searched for Richard. His sister had been close to a nervous collapse those first few days following the funeral.

"I woke up alone the next morning." She swallowed and wrapped her arms around her waist as if warding off a sudden chill. "He was gone. Without a word, without a note. Gone."

"When did you realize you were pregnant?"

"Six weeks later. I didn't know what to do. I was in denial and then in shock. It was horrible enough knowing I'd slept with a man who didn't care about me, who'd used me for his own purpose. Later, after a doctor confirmed the pregnancy, I had no way of contacting him to let him know."

"Did you think he'd leap up and offer to marry you?" Grady knew he sounded sarcastic, but couldn't restrain himself.

"No…but I thought he should know."

Grady said nothing, not wanting to ask the obvious question, and then he found it impossible to keep silent. "Does he know now? Is that why he took Maggie? Because he learned he had a child?"

"No!" she cried. "He knows nothing. I didn't even put his name on the birth certificate."

"Why'd he bring her back, then?"

"How should I know? But I'm grateful, terribly grateful, that he did."

So was Grady.

"Maggie's *my* child," Caroline said with open defiance. "There's none of her father in her."

Grady wanted to believe that. Now that he knew the truth though, it was obvious Maggie was his brother's child. Biologically, at any rate. Maggie had Richard's eyes and his dark hair.

"When he came back, did he try to pick up where you'd left off?" This was another one of those questions it hurt to ask because he feared the answer. And, he saw, another one of those questions that cut Caroline to the quick.

"No," she whispered. "When Richard first returned, I was terrified he'd figure out Maggie was his daughter and try to take her away from me. Don't you remember how I avoided the ranch after he first got home?" Her voice grew tight with remembered anxiety. "In the beginning I invented one excuse after another not to stop by. Every time I was near him I was afraid he'd say something about that night, and then I realized…" She paused, then covered her mouth with one hand and closed her eyes.

Grady's arms ached to hold her, but he remained where he was, steeling himself against her. "Realized what?"

"That…that he didn't even remember. I was just another face, another body. He'd used me the same way he'd used people his whole life. He might have suspected he'd…he'd been to bed with me, but he couldn't be sure, so he kept quiet."

"You're positive about that?"

"With Richard how can anyone be positive about anything? But it was just that one time and it was so long ago. I'm sure there've been a hundred women since."

They were silent for several moments before Grady spoke again. "Does anyone else know?"

She shook her head.

"Savannah?"

"I think she might have guessed, but we've never discussed the subject, and I've never come right out and told her.''

''Then·what makes you think Savannah's guessed?''

''I saw her look at Maggie once and then at Richard. Later I saw Richard's baby book in the kitchen and I knew she'd been comparing photographs.''

So his sister knew, which left Grady to wonder how many other people in Promise suspected. How many others were laughing at him behind his back?

Grady decided it was time to leave. He'd heard everything he could bear to listen to for one evening.

''Thank you for telling me. I know this wasn't easy— and I appreciate your honesty. You needn't worry—your secret is safe with me.''

''It wouldn't work, Grady,'' she said sadly, her eyes full of tears. ''I can see that now. It just wouldn't work with you and me.''

Then, weighed down by a sadness that seemed to encompass all the grief and despair he'd ever felt, he walked out the door. He had her answer. He loved her, had asked her to be his wife and she'd rejected him. Now he understood why.

''MOMMY,'' MAGGIE WHISPERED as Caroline lay on the living-room sofa, ''are you sick?''

''I'm fine, honey.''

''Then how come you're crying?''

''I'm sad, that's all,'' she said, discounting her pain for her daughter's sake.

''Why are you sad?'' Maggie pressed.

''There's a pain deep inside here,'' she said, flattening her hands over her heart.

''It's not going to bleed, is it?''

''No.'' Although a physical wound would be easier to endure.

In two days she hadn't heard from Grady, but then, she hadn't expected to. Twice Savannah had phoned, but Caroline had let her answering machine take the calls. She wasn't up to talking, even to her best friend.

"Are you going to bleed?" Maggie asked her again, her small face stiff with fear.

"No, Maggie. What makes you ask?"

The child didn't answer and Caroline slid over on the couch to give her room to sit down. The little girl curled up with her, and Caroline held her tight. It took a long time for the tension to leave Maggie's body. Eventually she drifted off to sleep and that, in Caroline's eyes, was a blessing.

Such a release didn't come for her, but she longed for it. At least when she was asleep, Grady's face wasn't there to haunt her. Awake, though, she couldn't escape the image of his shocked expression when he'd learned the truth.

The accusation, the blame, the disgust. By the time he left, he could barely tolerate being in the same room with her.

Caroline hugged Maggie, and to her amazement soon found herself drifting off. She must have slept because the next thing she knew, Maggie was shaking her shoulder with one hand and holding the portable telephone with the other.

"It's Savannah," she said.

Caroline could see it would be impossible to delay talking to her friend any longer. She sat up and took the receiver. 'Hi," she said, still groggy and slightly confused.

"It's Savannah. Are you all right?"

"I'm fine," she lied.

"If that's the case, why haven't you returned my calls?"

"I'm sorry, but I just didn't feel like talking."

Savannah hesitated, then blurted, "Good grief, what's the matter with you two? You sound as miserable as Grady."

Caroline had nothing to add to that.

"I'm coming over," her friend announced.

"Savannah, no! Please." But the line had already been disconnected and Caroline realized there was no help for it. Savannah Smith was a woman on a mission, and she wouldn't rest until she'd done whatever she could to straighten things out between these two people she loved. Two people who loved each other, according to Savannah. Well, she was right. Caroline did love Grady and was confident he loved her. Just not enough.

Knowing Grady's sister was coming to visit, Caroline washed her face and applied fresh makeup. The last thing she needed was for Savannah to return to the ranch with tales of Caroline pining away for want of Grady—however true that might be. She changed into a fresh shirt and jeans, then ran a comb through her hair.

Savannah arrived less than an hour later, storming into the house like an avenging angel. Caroline was ready with a fresh pitcher of iced tea, waiting for her in the sunny backyard patio. Maggie played contentedly in her sandbox, building castles with imaginary friends.

"All right," Savannah said, the minute they sat down. "What happened?"

"You mean Grady didn't tell you?"

Savannah gave a soft snicker and rolled her eyes. "All he'd say was that what happened is between you and him."

"He's right."

"I can't stand this, Caroline! He asked you to marry him, I know that much."

"He told you?"

"He didn't have to—I saw the diamond. Which means if he has it and you don't, you must've turned him down. But that doesn't make any sense. You love Grady."

Caroline said nothing.

"You *do* love him, don't you?"

"Yes." But that wasn't the issue.

"Then, Caroline, why would you reject him? I don't understand. I know it isn't any of my business, but it hurts me to see two people so obviously in love this unhappy."

Caroline didn't mean to start crying. The tears embarrassed her and she blinked rapidly, praying Savannah wouldn't notice. But of course she did and wasn't about to pretend otherwise.

Leaning forward, Savannah placed her hand on Caroline's arm. "Oh, Caroline, please tell me. I want to help."

"You can't. No one can."

Savannah wasn't so easily dissuaded. "You helped me when Laredo left, don't you remember? When he went back to Oklahoma, I was in so much pain I didn't know if I'd survive it, and you were there for me. It wasn't so much what you said, although I recall every word. It was your love and friendship that helped me through a horrible time. Let me help you now."

Caroline cupped the cold glass of iced tea with both hands. "He did ask me to marry him, and you're right, I refused."

"But why?"

"He…he said he was free to ask me because he was finished dealing with his brother's mistakes. Finished cleaning up after Richard." She inhaled and didn't exhale for several seconds. "I had to tell him. He has a right to know."

"About Maggie?" Savannah asked gently.

As Caroline suspected, Savannah had guessed that Richard was Maggie's father. She nodded.

"But why did you refuse his proposal?"

"I love Grady, but I don't want him to consider Maggie and me a burden. Just one more responsibility he's dealing with because of his brother. Another screwup in a long list."

"Doesn't Grady understand that Richard used you, too?"

"I'm not sure he does," she breathed. "It was too much of a shock."

Savannah sat back in her chair and tapped her finger against her lips. "Well, this certainly explains a great deal."

"Grady would feel I'd broken a confidence by discussing this with you," she felt obliged to remind her friend.

"You needn't worry about that."

"Why not?"

Savannah grinned. "My brother isn't speaking to me at the moment."

"Oh, Savannah."

"Not to worry. He isn't speaking to anyone."

So Grady wasn't taking this any better than she was. "He growls when one of us even dares to mention your name. Oh, and I heard him on the phone the other day. Apparently he was talking to Frank Hennessey because he said—or rather, shouted—that he wanted his bastard of a brother brought to justice."

"I take it there's no word about Richard?"

"None." Savannah shook her head. "It's as if he's vanished off the face of the earth, and at this point I don't really care. Richard deserves what he gets, as far as I'm concerned. Especially after this latest fiasco."

Caroline frowned, not understanding. "What fiasco?"

Savannah sighed. "He didn't tell you, did he?" She didn't wait for a response. "Grady can be too noble for his own good sometimes. Richard charged eight thousand dollars' worth of goods on the family accounts."

"No." Caroline felt sick to her stomach just knowing their brother was capable of something this underhand and cruel. Richard was well aware how long it had taken Grady to regroup after the family lost its money. Money stolen by

Richard. Then, just when Grady was financially able to get back on his feet, up popped Richard again. *Up pops the weasel.*

"He paid off every bill with his own money. Laredo and I wanted to share the expenses with him, but Grady refused. Seeing that we're newly married and building a home now, he wouldn't hear of it. Laredo wouldn't leave it at that— he said we're all partners and the money should come out of the business. But Grady said no. I don't have to tell you how stubborn he can be."

"You see?" Caroline said. "For the last six years all Grady's done is work to clean up Richard's messes. I'd just be one more."

"You don't honestly believe that, do you?"

"Yes, Savannah, I do."

"Then you don't know my brother." Savannah smiled slightly. "Give him time. Grady isn't that easily discouraged. He may need a few days to work things out, but he'll be back."

Caroline *wanted* to believe it, but she was afraid to hope.

"He loves you and Maggie. Mark my words, he isn't going to take no for an answer."

Caroline shook her head helplessly. She'd seen the pain in Grady's eyes, seen the shock and grief. She was just one more problem his brother had left behind, and he wanted out.

Caroline didn't blame him.

Chapter Eleven

Grady was in one bad mood. He'd been angry and cantankerous all week, to the point that he could barely stand his own company. Wiley said he'd rather chase strays than put up with Grady's foul temper and had left him to finish the repairs on the fence line by himself.

Grady had been doing the backbreaking work all afternoon, and although he'd managed to replace several rotting posts and make other fixes, his mind was a million miles away. Actually only about forty miles away. And while his hands were busy digging fence holes his thoughts were on Caroline.

"Damn it all to hell," he muttered and threw down the shovel. He'd finally finished for the day. Sweat poured from his brow, and his chest heaved from the physical exertion. "Damn it," he said again. He *should* be happy. The sale of the herd was scheduled and his financial problems would soon be over. Beef prices were up slightly. So why *wasn't* he happy? All he could think about was one headstrong woman who was too damn proud for her own good. What in the hell did she mean when she said a marriage between them wouldn't work? Why the hell not?

He could stand there stewing in the hot September sun or he could do something about it, Grady decided. Only he wasn't sure what. He tossed his tools into the back of the pickup, then drove at breakneck speed toward the house.

Savannah was working in her garden when he pulled into the yard. Her head was covered with a wide-brimmed straw hat, and she wore a sleeveless summer dress and an apron. The minute she spotted him she stepped out of the flower garden, a basket of freshly cut roses dangling from her arm.

"Grady?"

"Woman's a damn fool," he said, heading into the house. He took the porch steps two at a time. It didn't surprise him that his sister followed him inside; he would have been disappointed if she hadn't.

"I assume you're talking about Caroline," she said as she set the roses on the kitchen table.

"Is there anyone more stubborn than Caroline Daniels?" He paced the floor of the large kitchen, unable to stand still.

"Only one person I can think of," she said, smiling slightly. "And that's you."

"Me?" Grady considered himself a reasonable man. "Caroline rejected *me*. Not the other way around."

"Did she now?" Savannah removed a vase from the cupboard above the refrigerator. Grady recognized it as one that had belonged to their mother—crystal, sort of a bowl shape. He'd always liked it. Savannah began deftly arranging the roses.

"I asked Caroline to marry me," Grady said impatiently. He'd never intended to tell anyone what had happened, but the events of that evening burned inside him. It was either tell Savannah or scream it from the roof-top.

"So I understand," she murmured.

Grady had had it with women and their subtle messages. While he might normally have appreciated Savannah's reserved manner, it infuriated him just now.

"What exactly do you understand?" he demanded.

"Two hurting people, if you must know. Two people deeply in love with each other, neither one fully appreciating or—"

"She said no," he cut in. "She wasn't interested in being my wife—said it wouldn't work. Said it twice, as a matter of fact."

"Did she now?"

Grady slapped his hat against the edge of the counter. "If you have something to say, Savannah, just spit it out."

"Well, since you asked…" She gave him a demure smile. "It seems to me—and of course I could be wrong—that Caroline might have said no, but that wasn't exactly what she meant."

'I'm a simple rancher. If she said no and meant something else, then she should've come right out and *said* what she meant. I'm not a mind reader."

"Neither am I," Savannah stated. "But really, how else did you expect her to respond?"

"A yes would have sufficed."

"And what was she supposed to do then? Wait until your wedding day to casually mention that her child is also your niece?"

"No. It doesn't matter who fathered Maggie. I'm offering to be her daddy, to make her my own."

"Exactly!" Savannah rewarded him with a wide grin. "Bingo, big brother! Now collect your prize."

The woman was speaking in ridiculous riddles. "Damn it, Savannah, what do you mean by that?"

"You should be able to figure it out."

He frowned.

Savannah sighed loudly. "I believe what you said was, *It doesn't matter who fathered Maggie.* Now tell me, why is that?"

"Why?"

"Yes, why?" she repeated.

"Because I'm asking to be her father."

The smile was back in full force. "Very good, Grady." His frown deepened.

"You're almost there, big brother." She added a long-stemmed yellow rose to the vase.

"Almost? I've been there and back a thousand times in my mind. Why do I have to fall in love with the most stubborn woman in the entire state of Texas? What did I ever do to deserve this?"

"I don't know, but if I were you, I'd thank God every day of your life for a woman as wonderful as Caroline."

He stared at her.

"*If* you're lucky enough to convince her to be your wife, that is," Savannah said.

"As far as I'm concerned she has to come to me now." A man's pride could only take so much, and Caroline had run roughshod over it one time too many.

Savannah shook her head. "Wrong."

"Wrong?" Grady didn't see it like that, but he was desperate enough to listen to his sister's crazy reasoning.

"You were doing so well there, too," she said with another sigh. "Grady, I've never known you to be a man who took no for an answer. It's just not like you to roll over and play dead."

"I'm not playing dead!"

"You're just acting that way?" She made the statement a question, which irritated him even more.

"Either you don't love Caroline as much as I believe, or—"

"I love her and I love Maggie, too. When Maggie was missing, it felt as if a part of me was gone. When I saw she was safe and sound, I damn near broke into tears myself."

Savannah, ever patient, ever kind, beamed him a dazzling smile. "I'm not the one who needs to hear this, you know."

"So you're telling me I should ask Caroline again." Even as he spoke, he was shaking his head. "Not in this lifetime." In his view, it was Caroline's turn to risk her pride. If she wanted to change her mind, she could let him know. He grabbed his hat and walked out the back door.

"Where are you going?" his sister asked.

Until that moment he hadn't been sure, then in a flash he knew. "I'm going to give Caroline a chance to change her mind."

EDWINA AND LILY MOORHOUSE had just stepped up to the counter when the door to the post office flew open and Grady Weston stepped inside.

The two elderly women turned to look at him; so did Caroline. He was staring straight at her, and she could tell he was breathing fire.

"Caroline—"

She instantly returned her attention to the Moorhouse sisters. "Can I help you?" she asked ever so sweetly, ignoring Grady. Her heart was pounding like a frightened kitten's, but she refused, *refused,* to allow Grady to intimidate her.

"You can talk to the Moorhouse sisters until Kingdom come, and it isn't going to help. Eventually you're going to have to speak to me, too."

Edwina's eyes rounded as she glanced at her sister. "It's Grady Weston again."

"I have eyes in my head, sister. I can see it's Grady."

"Fit to be tied, from the looks of him."

"Indeed."

Despite the way her heart raced, Caroline found herself smiling.

"I do think he's constipated again, sister."

Lily studied him, tapping her foot. "Prunes, young man, eat prunes. They'll do wonders for your disposition."

Grady scowled at her, but Caroline knew it would take a lot more than that to intimidate the retired schoolteacher.

"Listen here, Grady Weston, I wiped your nose in third grade, so don't you be giving me dirty looks. My, oh my, but you always were a headstrong boy."

It was clear Grady wasn't going to be drawn into a verbal exchange with the two women.

"In some ways," Lily mused, "your stubbornness was a characteristic I admired."

Edwina slapped a ten-dollar bill onto the counter. "We'd like a book of stamps, Caroline."

"Of course." Caroline handed her the stamps with her change.

"Good day."

"Good day," Caroline replied, watching them leave.

"Good day, young man," Edwina said as she passed Grady and winked.

Caroline wasn't sure what to make of the wink. If Grady noticed it, he didn't let on.

He touched the brim of his hat and stepped around the two women in his rush to reach the counter.

"Can I help you?" Caroline asked, lowering her gaze for fear of what he might read in her eyes.

"As a matter of fact you can." Grady's voice echoed in the room.

She waited, figuring he wasn't going to ask for stamps.

"I'm here to talk some sense into you."

"Grady, listen—"

"Hear me out first. The last time we spoke I asked you to marry me and you turned me down."

Caroline doubted he'd ever fully comprehend how difficult it had been to reject him. She'd wanted to say yes more than anything she'd ever wanted in her life. But no self-respecting woman willingly entered a marriage if she believed she'd be a burden to her husband. Even loving him the way she did, she couldn't do that to him. Couldn't do it to herself.

"Be warned," he said, lowering his voice.

"Warned?"

"This time I'm not taking no for an answer."

"Grady, please…" He made this so damned hard.

"Sorry, it's too late for that. I don't want anyone but you."

She looked away rather than meet his gaze.

"For the past six years I've worked day and night and done without—just so I could make up for what we lost because of Richard. He's stolen six years of my life, Caroline. He's robbed me and Savannah of too much already, and I'll be damned if I'll let him rob me of anything else."

"I…I don't understand."

"If you allow Richard to stand between us now, it'll be one more thing my brother's taken from me. But this time I'm not the only person he's hurting. He's hurting you and Maggie, as well. Is that what you want?"

"No." Her voice sounded weak, unconvincing.

"You appear to have doubts."

"I… There's more than just me to consider," she said.

"Okay, let's talk about Maggie."

Slowly Caroline raised her eyes to his. Her daughter had to come first. Always. "What about Maggie?"

"I love her, too." It was the first time Grady had mentioned his feelings for her child, the first time he'd said this. "I'm looking to be more than your husband, Caroline. I'm looking to be Maggie's daddy."

She bit her lower lip.

"My brother might have fathered this child, but I'll be the one to raise her, to love her, to kiss her skinned knee.

I'll put her to bed at night, sit with her when she learns to read, teach her how to ride Moonbeam. Me, not Richard.''

It was a long speech for Grady, and every word was heartfelt. Caroline knew that in her bones, sensed it deep inside. They were the words of a man who understood that fatherhood was more than biological. Much more.

''Oh, Grady…''

''Is that all you have to say?''

''I—''

The door opened and Nell Bishop walked in with Jeremy and Emma. ''Hello,'' she said with a cheerful wave as she headed for her post-office box.

''Hello, Mr. Weston.''

''Howdy, Jeremy.''

''We're going swimming in the pool,'' Emma announced.

Nell sorted through her mail. ''Come on, you two,'' she said, and steered her children toward the door. She paused to look back at Grady and Caroline. ''Everything all right?'' she asked cautiously.

''Yes,'' Grady barked.

Caroline nodded.

Nell, who'd been married to a man as stubborn and lovable as the one standing there in front of her, smiled. ''Yes, I can see that everything is coming along nicely.'' Then she and her children left.

''What'd she mean by that?'' Grady demanded.

Caroline shrugged. ''You'll have to ask her.''

''Well?''

The gruff question caught her by surprise. ''Well, what?''

''Are you going to change your mind about marrying me or not?''

''I—''

''You're a fool if you turn me down.''

"Honestly, Grady—"

"You aren't likely to get a better offer."

This last comment irked her no end. "What makes you so sure?" she snapped. "Look, Grady," she began before he could answer, "let me ask you a question. Do you love me?"

"You know I do."

"You might have said so."

"I did," he insisted.

"When?"

"The first time I proposed."

"Oh." Well, that *was* true. But everything hinged on how *much* he loved her. "I'm afraid we'd be a burden to you."

"How?"

Caroline swallowed. "Every time you look at Maggie— and me—you'll be reminded of Richard. That's what I'm afraid of. We'd be just another problem Richard left for you to fix."

"That's not the way I see it, Caroline. I told you, re- member? I won't let Richard take another thing away from me. And you know what? For the first time in his life, my brother has given me something wonderful. He's hurt me, true, but he's also blessed me—in you. In Maggie."

"But—"

"Obviously the question is, do *you* love *me?*" he said. "You seem to be the one having trouble making up your mind."

"I love you so damn much," she confessed.

No sooner had the words left her lips than Grady reached across the counter for her. Their positions, the obstacle be- tween them, made the kiss awkward. It hardly mattered. They'd kissed countless times by now, but no kiss had ever meant this much.

It was a meeting of their hearts.

His mouth was warm and urgent against hers.

"We're getting married," he whispered.

"Yes," she whispered back. She whimpered when he deepened the kiss, then wrapped her arms around his neck and invited the exploration of his tongue.

The sound of someone entering the post office broke them apart. Caroline looked up guiltily, feeling a little shy.

Dovie Boyd stood in the foyer. She nodded toward them. "Hello, Grady. Caroline."

"Hi, Dovie," Caroline said, grateful Dovie wasn't a gossip. She shuddered to think of the consequences if someone like Louise or Tammy Lee had happened upon them in each other's arms.

"You're the first to hear our good news," Grady said, taking Caroline's hand. He grasped it firmly in his own, then raised it to his lips. "Caroline has agreed to be my wife."

Dovie's eyes grew wide. "Congratulations! I couldn't be happier." She opened her purse and took out a linen handkerchief. "I really...couldn't...be...happier," she said, sniffling and dabbing at her eyes. "You're a wonderful couple and...and I think it's just wonderful, really I do." She turned abruptly and walked out, apparently forgetting what had brought her to the post office in the first place.

GRADY, CAROLINE and Maggie sat on the front-porch swing. "Will I call you Daddy?" Maggie asked Grady.

"Of course. If you want to."

She nodded. "Then I'll have a daddy, too."

"Yes, princess, you'll have a daddy."

"And Mommy will have a husband."

"And Grady'll have a family." He tucked his arm around Caroline's shoulder, loving her so much.

"Us," Maggie said, and tossed her arms in the air. "Your family is us."

"What do you think of that?" Caroline asked her daughter.

Maggie considered the question a moment, looked up at Grady and slowly grinned. "You don't do magic tricks," she said, "but I like you better 'cause you love me and Mommy."

"That," Grady said, kissing the top of her head, "is very true. You're both very easy to love."

"I'm glad you think so," Caroline whispered and leaned her head against his shoulder, utterly content.

* * * * *

*In DR. TEXAS Jane Dickinson continues
her lessons in life, Texas-style—which include
falling in love: Find out how things are going for
new marrieds Glen & Ellie Patterson…and for
Savannah and Laredo, who are in for a surprise.
Then there's Richard—how long can he last at
Bitter End? Meanwhile, Dovie and Frank
come in for their share of heartbreak;
is there any solution to their emotional impasse?
Join your friends in Promise next month!*

MILLS & BOON®

Next Month's Romance Titles

♡

Each month you can choose from a wide variety of romance novels from Mills & Boon®. Below are the new titles to look out for next month from the Presents™ and Enchanted™ series.

Presents™

THE MISTRESS ASSIGNMENT	Penny Jordan
THE VIRGIN BRIDE	Miranda Lee
THE SEDUCTION GAME	Sara Craven
ONE WEDDING REQUIRED!	Sharon Kendrick
LUC'S REVENGE	Catherine George
THE MARRIAGE TAKEOVER	Lee Wilkinson
THE PLAYBOY'S BABY	Mary Lyons
HIRED WIFE	Karen van der Zee

Enchanted™

BOARDROOM PROPOSAL	Margaret Way
DR. TEXAS	Debbie Macomber
THE NINE-DOLLAR DADDY	Day Leclaire
HER HUSBAND-TO-BE	Leigh Michaels
THE FATHERHOOD SECRET	Grace Green
A WIFE AND CHILD	Rosemary Carter
A REAL ENGAGEMENT	Marjorie Lewty
WIFE WITHOUT A PAST	Elizabeth Harbison

On sale from 2nd April 1999

H1 9903

Available at most branches of WH Smith, Tesco, Asda, Martins, Borders, Easons, Volume One/James Thin and most good paperback bookshops

Enchanted™

★ SONS OF ★
PROMISE

DEBBIE MACOMBER

If you have enjoyed meeting the
characters in this book, look out for them
again next month in:

Dr. Texas

and again in:

May—Nell's Cowboy
June—Lone Star Baby

MILLS & BOON®

Makes any time special™

MILLS & BOON®

A man for mum!

Mills & Boon® makes Mother's Day
special by bringing you three new
full-length novels by three of our
most popular Mills & Boon authors:

Penny Jordan
Leigh Michaels
Vicki Lewis Thompson

On Sale 22nd January 1999

MILLS & BOON®

Makes any time special™

By Request

Bestselling themed romances brought back to you by popular demand

Each month By Request brings you three full-length novels in one beautiful volume featuring the best of the best.

So if you missed a favourite Romance the first time around, here is your chance to relive the magic from some of our most popular authors.

Look out for
***Sole Paternity* in March 1999 featuring Miranda Lee, Robyn Donald and Sandra Marton**

Available at most branches of WH Smith, Tesco, Asda, Martins, Borders, Easons, Volume One/James Thin and most good paperback bookshops

FREE

4 BOOKS
AND A SURPRISE GIFT!

We would like to take this opportunity to thank you for reading this Mills & Boon® book by offering you the chance to take FOUR more specially selected titles from the Enchanted™ series absolutely FREE! We're also making this offer to introduce you to the benefits of the Reader Service™ —

★ FREE home delivery
★ FREE monthly Newsletter
★ FREE gifts and competitions
★ Exclusive Reader Service discounts
★ Books available before they're in the shops

Accepting these FREE books and gift places you under no obligation to buy; you may cancel at any time, even after receiving your free shipment. Simply complete your details below and return the entire page to the address below. **You don't even need a stamp!**

YES! Please send me 4 free Enchanted books and a surprise gift. I understand that unless you hear from me, I will receive 6 superb new titles every month for just £2.40 each, postage and packing free. I am under no obligation to purchase any books and may cancel my subscription at any time. The free books and gift will be mine to keep in any case.

N9EC

Ms/Mrs/Miss/Mr ....Initials ....
BLOCK CAPITALS PLEASE

Surname...

Address..

....

....Postcode ....

Send this whole page to:
THE READER SERVICE, FREEPOST CN81, CROYDON, CR9 3WZ
(Eire readers please send coupon to: P.O. Box 4546, DUBLIN 24.)

mps MAILING PREFERENCE SERVICE

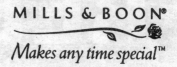

MILLS & BOON®

Makes any time special™

The Regency
Collection

Mills & Boon® is delighted to bring back, for a limited period, 12 of our favourite Regency Romances for you to enjoy.

These special books will be available for you to collect each month from May, and with two full-length Historical Romance™ novels in each volume they are great value at only £4.99.

Volume One available from 7th May